MW00574041

WOMEN LIE MEN LIE - PART 3

A. ROY MILLIGAN

CHAPTER 1

*G*loria finished punching her code in and noticed JC jumping in his sleep. "What's wrong?"

JC jumped up and grabbed her arm, "Nothing...Nothing," he said, shaking his head trying to get the image out his mind.

"You look sick, are you ok?"

"Nah I'm straight, just a fucked up dream." He looked around. "So you live with the white people huh? This is nice. You living good!"

"Thanks, I try to do my best. I was raised in a little old shack outside of Atlanta, the other side of Atlanta. Lived with my three sisters in one room. I always swore that when I grew up I was gonna have me a big house with a room all to myself. Even when I got a man with me, I still save a room for just me in case I get claustrophobic or something."

"Wow, well you made it. Look at these houses. They must cost millions!" JC commented, whistling softly under his breath.

They pulled up to Gloria's house and he was blown away by the detailed architecture outside, the immaculate landscaping, the vibrant colors of the flowers that skirted the edges. *Yeah, I made the right choice calling her*, he thought to himself.

They got out when she parked in the garage and motioned to the back, "Those are the stairs to your room. I have the sheets changed each week by a maid that comes out weekly, so they should be fresh, let me know if it ain't, I'll fire her. You want to come in and have something to eat? Because I'm beat, but I can make something. There's no food in the fridge up there but we can fix that tomorrow."

JC grabbed his bag of money and started to walk up the stairs, "Yeah, give me a minute to check things out and I'll meet you inside," he told her as he walked up to the door and opened it. Gloria went through the lower door that connected the garage to her place. JC was still thinking of Kelly and Merido, wondering if he dreamed it? Was it a sign that they were coming or his own conscience playing with him? He pulled his gun out and checked the place out carefully before relaxing. The bed was queen sized with a dark blue comforter. The dresser was of good quality as was the walnut brown, leather recliner in the corner underneath a metal reading light. It had a dark wood floor with a multi-colored carpet to keep your feet from getting cold in the morning, and a decent size tub and shower combo. The fridge was small, but big enough for just him sitting next to the sink and microwave. Not bad, he had lived in worse places than this. He heard Gloria calling his name from below, so he decided to wait until later to check everything else out. He stashed his money underneath the recliner and went downstairs where she had made them big turkey sandwiches. There were side plates of cheese, tomatoes, and lettuce along with mustard and mayo.

"I wasn't sure what you liked, so I pulled out a little of everything I hope it's okay. You want something to drink? I got beer, water, and a little of this koolaid, watermelon and mango?"

"Damn, for real? That's my favorite koolaid, you like that shit, too?"

"Nah, I got it as a promo thing when my store was having a sale. My housekeeper likes it though."

JC started to make a couple of sandwiches while she stirred him a container of koolaid. JC walked up behind her and poured two more spoons of sugar in the mixture, saying, "I like it real sweet."

Gloria turned around and was inches from his face. "You do?" she asked licking her lips in preparation for the kiss she knew was coming.

"Uh, huh. Real sweet." he could tell she wanted him to kiss her, but he was making her wait.

JC took a sip of the glass and said, "Mmmm, that's just about right. You want a sip?"

Gloria nodded her head and waited while he tilted the glass for her, and she let the sweet concoction drip down her throat. At the moment it was the most delicious thing she had ever tasted. "That is good."

JC leaned in and kiss her top lip softly, then her bottom lip, "You taste sweet, too," he said sucking her lips, then sliding the tip of his tongue in her mouth, pulling out when hers sought his out. He was unwilling to let her have control, he wanted her to want him, badly.

Gloria waited for what was coming next and she was dreading turning him down because he tasted so good, and he kissed like he had the lips of a God. His hands felt like tempered steel, hot and hard as they stroked her body, under and around the sides of her tits, down her ass, to her thighs. She could feel herself getting wet and knew she hadn't taken a bath all day, making her feel embarrassed and self-conscious, but she didn't want him to stop. *Carry me into the bedroom and fuck me, JC,* she thought to herself.

JC knew she wanted him and probably thought she was gonna get his dick, but he needed her to more than just want him, he needed her to need him.

"Thank you for coming to get me," he said, kissing her neck and earlobes.

"You're welcome, JC," she said, breathlessly.

"I'll see you in the morning," he said, giving her one more kiss, planting his tongue inside her mouth while letting his dick poke into her so she felt the girth of his package.

Gloria was surprised that he said that, wondering if he was playing some kind of game. "Okay, I'll see you in the morning, JC. Sleep tight."

"You too, dream of me." He grabbed his sandwiches and koolaid and went upstairs, not even bothering to look to see if she was watching him, he knew she was.

When he got upstairs and sat down. He turned on the TV and ate his food before calling it a night at just past nine. The sun wasn't fully down yet, but it was enough for him to shut the lights off and fall asleep, gun still in his hand.

He woke up in the morning to a knock at the door and Gloria's voice. "JC, you up?"

JC pulled the sheet over his body, wearing only a pair of boxers and said, "Come on in,"

4

Gloria had a tray full of breakfast items. "Don't get all excited because I sure as hell didn't make this. I don't have time to be cooking, but there's a place not to far from here, that makes amazing breakfast trays for delivery."

JC stopped being modest and stood up six pack glistening in the morning sun as well as the morning hardness of his dick. He made sure Gloria got a good look before he put his sweatpants and shirt on. He went into the bathroom and gargled some mouthwash, then he went to the table and gave Gloria a kiss on her lips, "Good morning, thanks for breakfast. It's the thought that counts not who made it," he said, digging in.

"So listen, I have to go to a couple of my shops and pick up some money, but maybe you'd like to get a couple of outfits before we go there. I'm sure you dress a lot different, right?"

"Yeah, I had a slight wardrobe malfunction with my other hook-up. I could use a make over that's for sure. When you ready give me a holla, and we'll get to it."

"Whenever you're done eating we can go," she said, surprising him, because he thought she was going to lay around for a minute, but she was all business, which is something he liked.

Gloria drove him around the city of Atlanta which was busy, busier than Detroit at this time of day. It was beautiful in the daylights after the fog had lifted, and it was already warm. Gloria took him to an upscale shop that catered to men, letting him try some things on while she made phone calls and worked on her laptop. The sale's clerks brought her latte's and cream filled pastries while he bought two outfits, one for hanging out and another for going out. Gloria nodded her head in approval, happy he had a sense of style, she wouldn't be embarrassed by

5

him. Then they went to three shops of hers, JC knew she was flaunting him around as eye candy for her employees. She introduced them all to JC, making sure they knew he was with her, as if her arm entwined in his didn't already say that to them.

CHAPTER 2

"*Wow*, you a busy girl, huh? I'm impressed, Gloria. Most girls ain't got it going on like this, you doing real well, huh?"

"Yeah, guess I'm doing okay. I could be doing better, but I got some other things happening. Look, JC, I wanted to talk to you about something, while you was in the bathroom, I called a friend of mine, she's a doctor. I thought you might like to get checked out."

"Checked out? I ain't sick! Why I need a doctor?"

Gloria didn't know how to approach him because usually she knew a guy for awhile before letting him know she was kind of OCD about diseases. "Uhmm, I'm just gonna be straight with you, JC. I like you, and I think we get along real well, but I have this thing. It's not a big deal, but any guy I might be with, I need him to be checked out for anything."

"What you mean, anything? You think I got something?"

"No, nothing like that. You'd be surprised how often people don't get checked for STD'S until it's too late. So I'm actually doing you a favor. Is this weird?" she asked, feeling like an idiot.

"It's okay. I know what you saying. I appreciate you looking out for me. I'll do it for you, because I like you," JC said, moving over and kissing Gloria's lips softly, as his tongue slipped into her mouth for a second. One of her employees whistled, making her blush. "Besides, I have to be honest with you, I want to have a baby at some point. I ain't getting any younger and I want my kid to have a woman like you for a mother. Someone who has her mind tight and her shit together."

"Wow, I don't think a guy has ever said that to me. Most man are terrified of the baby talk, but you just come out with it."

"That's how we do in Michigan, ain't no reason to beat around the bush, right?"

"Oh my." Was all Gloria could say when the kiss ended. Her heart started beating really fast when he said he wanted a baby, which is what she had been wanting for awhile, but not just with anyone. "Let's get you checked out!" she said, smiling brightly and grabbing her purse.

"Damn, you gonna let a nigga finish his lunch?" JC asked with a smile.

"Sorry," Gloria said, laughing as she sat back down and waited impatiently for him to finish so they could get to the good parts.

Hours later, Gloria and JC were on their way to a nearby clinic. Gloria knew she would have sex with him if they slept in the same bed, so she wanted to get him tested for any STD's. She didn't want some other girl's diseases crawling into her body. Luckily, she knew a doctor at a discrete clinic that didn't ask any questions, provided you were willing to pay for that

WOMEN LIE MEN LIE - PART 3

discretion. Otherwise, they would have to go through the formality of asking for JC's real name and to see proof of it on an ID. Instead, the clinic simply had JC go into a private room when they arrived. Once he was settled in, Gloria left to run some quick errands.

The exam room was pretty standard, filled with sterile stainless steel, boring wall colors, and the smell of antiseptic resinated in the air. The cabinets and drawers were filled with gloves, gauze boxes, tongue depressors, and empty vials for blood draws. JC looked up nervously when the door opened, expecting to see some old indian guy in a white coat. He was pleasantly surprised to see a short woman come in who looked mixed with white and Mexican. She was an attractive woman with a mole on the side of her left cheek. It gave her an appeal that he found sexy. Her almond-colored hair was cut into a cute bob with blonde highlights. She wore a stethoscope around her neck and a mini flashlight in her front pocket. Her white doctor's coat covered up a yellow dress that was conservative enough to not be frowned upon. Her breasts were on the small side, but firm and the nipples were standing at attention as they struggled to be free of the dress she wore.

"Hi, I'm Carren, a close friend of Gloria's. Sorry it took so long to see you, but it was last minute when Gloria called and I was in the middle of stitching up a wound," she explained, reaching her hand out to shake JC's.

JC caressed her hand instead of shaking it, looking into her chocolate eyes as he said, "I'm JC, it's nice to meet you Carren."

Pointing to a small metal-framed bed that reclined like a seat against the wall, Carren said, "Okay, I need you to stand over there for me. When was the last time you saw a doctor or have been tested for STD's?"

9

Not feeling as embarrassed as before, JC replied honestly, "It's been awhile."

"Really?" Carren asked, kind of shocked that people were so blasé about STD's, AIDS, and Herpes. "You have to keep up on your check-ups. There's a lot of diseases going around and trust me, you don't want to be the victim. I see people come and go out of here every day with diseases and yet they still don't wear condoms."

"Well, now I have you looking out for me. So I'll call you when I feel sick."

Carren kind of snorted out a laugh as she put on a pair of sterile gloves.

"I'm serious! Can I call you if I feel sick or show any symptoms?" JC asked.

Carren thought about his question for a few seconds while she prepared to check him. She wondered if he was hitting on her or being serious. It was hard to tell these days, either way she appreciated his efforts. "Uhmm, just contact Gloria if you need to see me," she decided.

"Gloria? Why do I need to contact Gloria to see a doctor? You're the doctor, right?"

"Yes, I am. But I've also known Gloria for a long time and I don't want any drama interfering with our business arrangements, that's all." Carren explained, hoping he wouldn't push too much further or she might just give in.

"That's all good, but this is my health we're talking about. Gloria doesn't have to know. Don't you have an oath to follow or something? It's just a number Carren."

Carren took a deep breath, trying to regain her composure. "I don't know about that JC. Let's just get on with the procedure.

I need you to drop your pants and drawers for me. Then lie back please."

"Let me get this straight. You won't give me your number, but you want me to drop my pants on the first date, and without a condom in sight?" JC asked, grinning mischievously at her.

Carren laughed and said, "Come on Prince Charming, follow my directions and we'll get you out of here soon enough."

JC did as she asked and noticed Carren's pupils getting larger when he dropped his pants and showed her the package. She held her composure pretty well, but JC knew that with a little bit more work, he would have her. He was able to read her body just fine, and he could tell she liked what she saw dangling between his legs.

"Please don't hurt me Doc," he said, mockingly as she grabbed his dick in her hand, standing it straight up and placing a swab into his urethra.

"You're going to feel a small sting coming...right...now," she said moving the swab deeper into his dick.

11

CHAPTER 3

"*S*hiittt....," he exclaimed, feeling the sting all over his tense body. His eyes clenched shut as she swirled the tip around for a few seconds.

Even though the procedure was over fairly quickly and with little discomfort, it still was not a pleasant experience. Carren placed the swab into a vial and left to test the swab and was back within ten minutes with the results. "Congratulations! The good news is that your results are all negative but just to be safe, I'd like to take some blood for an HIV test..."

JC interrupted her in mid-sentence, "I appreciate that, but the HIV test is the one thing I have been tested recently for. In the last thirty days to be exact."

"Then you're all set, JC. Hopefully you'll continue to wear condoms and save me the trouble of having to test you again. I'm sure you don't want a repeat of that stinging sensation, it doesn't get any easier."

"How can I get in touch with you again? This is my first time in Atlanta and I don't really know anyone. I have a feeling you'd be a real good tour guide," he said, laying it on thick for her with an obvious insinuation.

Carren smiled and blushed a little at the compliment, but said, "Contact Gloria if you need to see me."

"Why you doing me like this?"

"Like what?" Carren asked.

"Like I can't call you for help. Who else can I call, if not a doctor?"

Carren's barriers fell, lying to herself that it was only in case he did need medical help. But she admitted to herself that she did like him. "Okay, you can call me, but only for help. That's it, JC!" she added while writing her personal number down on the back of the clinic's business card.

JC grabbed the card into his hand like a well deserved trophy and asked, "You married?"

"No, I'm not married. Why do you ask that?"

"Why aren't you?"

"JC, this examination is over," she said firmly, walking out the door, not even bothering to answer his question. *Men are all the same*, she thought.

JC knew he was playing with fire by getting her number, but he didn't care. He needed to meet as many new females as he could, he never knew when his good thing with Gloria would end. The whole state was foreign to him. Everything was different, especially the girls. They all had these sexy ass southern accents that he found irresistible.

After Gloria picked him up and found out the results, she took JC to eat at a fancy restaurant to celebrate, but the meal was smothering them both as they stared across the table at each other. Finding reasons to touch one another, barely tasting the exquisite and expensive dishes that arrived every few minutes. The waiter was professional despite the obvious sexual tension that existed at his table. He attended to their needs quickly and efficiently, giving them the space and privacy they desperately wanted. When it came time for dessert, they chose to skip sweets for the anticipated one that would be served when they got back home.

As soon as they stepped inside the foyer of Gloria's place, JC slammed her against the wall and firmly pressed his mouth against hers, forcing his tongue past her sultry lips. He palmed her voluptuous backside aggressively with both hands, massaging it firmly, then gently. When his hand slid up her beige skirt, Gloria slapped at him playfully before grabbing his hand and leading him to her bedroom upstairs.

JC pushed her back as she sunk into the soft California king-sized bed. She laid there feeling a bit high, even though she wasn't, as JC stripped the clothes from her. Gloria thought briefly about getting up and dancing or stripping for him, but his nimble fingers slid the clothes from her effortlessly. Once her clothes could no longer hide her curves from him, JC began sucking her pink, perfectly manicured toes one by one. He licked and caressed her feet as if she were Cleopatra and he were Marc Anthony. JC then moved up to her ankles, past the scar on her calf where a dog had bit her as a child. Then to the inner part of her thigh, pausing at the strawberry colored birthmark on her right leg. He worked his way up to her titties, sucking and massaging her breasts until she let out a delicious sounding moan. Her eyebrows tilted towards each other with passion and her cute little nose scrunched up while her hand cupped the back of his dedicated and busy head. He crawled between her legs and kissed her lips gently, letting their tongues intertwine like two vipers mating. "Be gentle with me," she whispered in his ear, almost like a secret rather than a real plea.

JC kissed her and slid inside of her slowly, letting her pussy accept him past the velvety inner lips. Her insides were like a puddle, wet and dripping. Although her pussy felt good, something was off, almost awkward. Gloria didn't really move with him, moan at all, or grab at his body. Not like she had done when he was kissing her. She laid limp like a mannequin at a shopping mall, looking good, but offering very little in the way of compensation or reciprocation. He didn't stop though. He continued to stroke her body slowly, then he sped up without warning and became more aggressive, hoping to inspire her to respond. He pulled his dick out of her and turned her body to the side and inserted his dick back in, pounding away non-stop until Gloria began shouting, "Ahh, ah, ahhh!"

He fucked her for 15 minutes in the same position before he turned her onto her stomach, doggie style. "Arch your back," he ordered, before sticking his dick inside, but her back wasn't arched right. "Arch it," he yelled, smacking her on the right side of her ass.

"Ouch! That hurt, JC!"

"Then arch that back," he commanded, pressing his hand down on the center of her back.

"Okay, shit," she said, finally with his demand and arching the way he wanted.

JC, while thrusting his dick in and out, noticed her head was hanging down like she had no interest in being involved. So JC grabbed her by the hair and asked, "What's wrong with you?"

"Nothing, why?" she asked, as he slowed down.

"Throw that ass back then and act like you want this shit," he ordered her before jamming his dick inside her.

Gloria started moving a little, that's when JC finally figured out that she had no rhythm, so he took control and grabbed her by the waist. He started beating her pussy until he nutted. When he pulled his dick out, it was covered with her cum. He had no idea she even had an orgasm. *This bitch is weird*, he thought to himself. Gloria was lucky she had money or he would never fuck her again. JC laid down next to her getting his breath back and was on the verge of falling asleep when her voice jolted him into consciousness.

"JC? You up?" she asked, lying next to him, still naked.

"Yeah, what's up?" he asked, hoping she wasn't going to get all weepy or sentimental on him.

"Carren told me you asked for her number."

CHAPTER 4

*J*C let the silence sit for a few seconds before responding, "And?"

"And, she's my friend! What you mean, and?"

"She's a doctor, I asked for her number in case I had any symptoms or anything. I thought you wanted me to be clean and checked out?" JC said, thinking fast, not surprised that Carren ratted him out.

"So that's the only reason you asked for her number?"

"Yea, Gloria. That's it! Why else would I ask for some stuck up ass doctor's number?"

"Okay, I'm going to trust you until you give me a reason not to," Gloria said naively, hoping he wouldn't end up acting like every other guy she had trusted.

"Now can I get some sleep?"

"Yes…how was it?" she asked after a few seconds of silence.

"How was what? The physical?"

"No, the sex?"

Her question threw him for a loop, so he responded with, "Oh...it was good," he lied, "Best shit ever!"

Gloria smiled from ear to ear and said, "I told you! Now nigga, don't be acting all crazy trying to hit this shit whenever you want!"

"Don't worry, I won't," he said, trying his hardest not to laugh in her face and tell her she was horrible. JC knew he was going to have to find some other females to have sex with down in Atlanta, because Gloria's sex game wasn't nearly up to par yet. And her pussy wasn't all that either. He expected her to be tighter than she was.

The next morning when JC woke up, he mounted Gloria as she was sleeping and began fucking her awake until he nutted inside her. He wanted kids and so did she, so it was no big deal to either of them. Although her sex game was still wack as hell, he planned to teach her some moves later on. Right now though, he wanted her to think she was the best he ever had.

Gloria got out of bed with a fresh glow and walked naked towards the bathroom with her pussy making a squishing noise with every step.

"Is that you farting or your pussy?"

Gloria laughed and said, "I don't use that P word! That's my Va-J-J, thank you very much!"

When JC heard the water running in the shower he got up and started searching her room. He didn't trust people and if he had to sleep here, he wanted to feel somewhat safe. He would have to keep his gun and put it somewhere within arm's reach for when he was sleeping. After looking in her closets and dresser drawers and he didn't find any guns, knives, or cameras hidden anywhere. He sat back on the bed and observed her compulsively neat room. The furniture was tastefully expensive. Slightly old fashioned from the modern look he was used to with dark wood and cream colored paint and drapes. His thoughts turned to Brittany and the way she decorated. He recalled all the time they had spent together. He missed Brittany so much, and the more he thought of her, the sadder he felt. So sad that tears began to leak from his eyes. He surprised himself with the pent-up emotion. He wasn't immune to crying, but it had been a long time since he cried especially over a girl. Without warning the water turned off in the bathroom and with no time to prepare himself, Gloria exited the bathroom naked and dripping water onto the carpet. He tried to dry his tears as fast as possible before she saw them, but he was too late.

"What's wrong? Are you crying, baby?" she asked.

"No, no, nah...hell nah. Something just flew in my damn eye!"

"Come here bay, let me blow in it," she said, kneeling in front of him.

"Nah, I got it now," he said, still drying the tears away.

"You ready for some more then?" she asked, standing up with her belly in his face.

"Damn, girl. You want more?" he asked, a little surprised and still thinking of Brittany.

"If we gonna make a baby, we gotta get to it, right?" she asked, straddling his dick on the bed.

After twenty minutes of having to force her to perform, they finished with the sex. They took a quick shower together then got dressed. Making him realize how dependent he was on Gloria, a feeling he didn't like. He needed to find a hustle of some kind.

"I wanna go to the mall," he said, walking into her office that had a sliding door looking outside onto the terrace.

Without bothering to look up from the computer where she was checking her e-mails, she said, "I will when I get back."

"When you coming back? Where you going?" he asked, feeling ridiculous asking about her.

"I need to make rounds at my coffee shops. I also have to pick up a friend of mine and drop her off where she needs to go."

"How long that's gone take?"

"Why? You got somewhere you gotta be?" she asked suspiciously thinking of what Carren had said.

"Nowhere. I'm just asking. I don't want to be sitting around here all day while you out and about. But go ahead, let me know when you on the way back." he explained quickly so he didn't get her pissed and he'd really be stuck.

Gloria was on her way to the businesses she owned when she saw a friend of hers getting out of her car. Her friend, Juicy. She was a really good friend of Gloria, who was actually a stripper who made a ton of money dancing for men. "Hey, girl! Why didn't you call me? I'm on my way to pick up Lindsay right now," Gloria yelled out, as she rolled down the car window.

"I don't know. I know I should have, but I got distracted girl. You know me!" Juicy exclaimed with a big smile plastered across her face. Juicy was by all definitions, pretty. She was only 24 years old living in Atlanta alone. She drove a midnight blue Challenger SRT and lived in a decked out apartment. She didn't need a man to take care of her, which is why her and Gloria got along so well.

"I need to talk to you about something. Lock up your car and come with me, unless you gotta be somewhere," Gloria asked, pulling up to the curb so Juicy could get in.

"No, I'm free right now. Where we going besides to get Lindsay?" Juicy asked, as she climbed inside Gloria's Bentley and reclined the seat all the way back. Not that she needed leg room to accommodate her 5'6" red-boned frame. Juicy had a tiny waist that Gloria admired, a big old booty, which is where her name Juicy came from. She had breast implants that would make any Hollywood star jealous, and long blonde hair that draped past her shoulders. Juicy kept in good shape stripping, but she also taught pole dancing classes to the suburban moms trying to keep their men. Her classes were off the charts and people signed up weeks in advance to take one of her classes.

"You look super cute girl," Gloria commented, looking at the skin tight tan sun dress she wore that was a bit too long to be considered a mini, but not long enough to wear to church. She wore a see-through, white silk blouse with a white lace bra underneath. Her ears dripped in white gold holding a one carat diamond at the end and her feet were encased in knee high boots on four inch heels. A very dramatic look that she went for.

CHAPTER 5

"*T*hanks, girl. You look nice, too. Why you look so happy? You can't even stop smiling. What have you been doing?" Juicy asked, happy to see her girl smiling for once. She worked way too hard.

Gloria couldn't help but smile bigger. "I have me a new man, that's all!" she said, spilling it out all at once, she couldn't even keep Juicy in suspense.

"Who girl? Do I know him? He got a friend for me? Hook a sista' up!"

"Nope, he ain't from around here. And he ain't got no friends, but I want you to meet him and tell me what you think," Gloria said, knowing Juicy had a player radar for someone trying to get down on a girl because she had money.

"Where did you meet him? And please don't say the club!" Juicy asked, knowing her friend's reputation for picking up young, broke ass fools from the clubs in and around Atlanta.

Gloria took a deep breath and said, "It's a long story, but let's just say…a rest area."

"Fair enough...and? You know I need more details than that."

"He's from Michigan and I don't know a whole lot about him, besides he's fine as hell and he wants kids. Oh, you might not be interested in this little tidbit, but he can fuck too!" Gloria gloated, causing them both to break out into laughter.

"He sounds like a winner so far. What's them pockets looking like?"

"I don't need his money, I got my own. But he's okay. Matter of fact, let me call him real quick," Gloria said, getting a little defensive about the money question. Juicy was always telling her not to settle for some broke ass nigga and to find a guy who had his own thing going on. But that was easier said than done. Gloria didn't want some stuck-up black Republican who walked and talked like a white boy from the suburbs.

Gloria dialed her home phone hoping JC answered. But he didn't so she started talking through the answering machine. "It's me, Gloria! JC, pick up the phone, please."

"Hello?" JC's deep voice asked as he answered the phone.

"Hey, do you want me to shop for you and you can pay me back when I get home?" Gloria asked, showing off for her friend that she was in a real relationship.

"Pay you back? What you mean, pay you back?"

"JC, don't be silly."

"I ain't being silly, but you got shit fucked up. If we supposed to be together why would I pay you back for anything? You on some other shit, bye!" he said, hanging up on her.

"No that nigga didn't!" Gloria said, looking at the phone, not believing it said, 'call ended'.

"What?" Juicy asked, while applying eye liner in the sun visor mirror.

"Nothing," Gloria replied while calling JC back. She didn't get an answer right away so she was left with the humiliating experience of talking into the answering machine again in front of Juicy. "I'm sorry, JC. We must have got disconnected. You right, I got you baby. Don't worry about nothing. I'm going to get you all the way together, but I need you to pick up so I can get your sizes."

JC picked up after making her stew for a minute then gave her his sizes. Plus, he told her to buy some dumb bells for him to work out with and have them delivered to the house today. Gloria agreed and apologized once more, before realizing JC had hung up on her in mid-apology.

Juicy heard enough to know they argued about something, but she tried to be supportive and said, "You must really like him girl."

"Shut up, Juicy! I'm trying to be nice and help him out until I can find out what he's like," Gloria explained while driving and thinking about JC.

"You know what I want you to do, Juicy?"

"What?"

"I want you to test him for me. I want you to go over there while I'm shopping and see if you can seduce him. If he fucks you, at least you get a good fuck then I'm back on the dating block looking for his replacement."

"What? That's the craziest thing I have ever heard from you. Why you gotta test him? Why would you do that to him? You know how simple-minded men are, following their dicks all the time. You shouldn't have to test your man, either he's a cheater or he's not!"

"Yeah, but he's young! Probably around your age, and I want to be sure about him before I invest any time or money. And I do know how men are, which is why I'm sending you in. If he don't fuck you, he can withstand any hoochie mama that comes his way."

"Damn, Gloria! That's some twisted ass shit! But remember, he is still just a man!"

"I know, but will you do it for me?"

"Do what? Have sex with your man?"

"Well, try to anyway," Gloria stated, hoping he wouldn't disappoint her.

"Girl, there ain't no trying! Can't no man resist this booty when I get to spinning on his pole! He's going to want all of this if I try to give it to him. Just don't be getting all mad at me if he hits it," Juicy said, blowing a kiss at herself in the mirror after putting on lipstick.

Gloria laughed at her friend's kissy faces and replied, "Whatever! He might pass on that! Nah, I'm just playing."

"Well, I'm still on my period. Can it wait? I should be done tomorrow or the next day."

"I thought you was on birth control? What happened?"

"That shit was fucking up my cycles, but I'm going back on the shot in a few weeks though. I shouldn't have gotten off it in the first place," Juicy commented, distracted by a shirtless guy riding on a motorcycle in the next lane.

"So when you get off your period will you do it for me?" Gloria asked, pressing the issue.

"Yeah, I got you girl. But be careful what you ask for, you might not like the results," Juicy warned her friend.

"That's why I love you girl. You be keeping it real," Gloria said, noticing her phone was vibrating. "Remind me to show you these pictures when I get off the phone."

"Okay, you know I want to see what I'm going to be working with."

"Hello?" Gloria asked, laughing as she spoke into the phone.

"What's up, honey? You laughing at me?" a foreign sounding voice on the other end asked. It was Lamoto, a guy she trafficked millions of dollars for on a monthly basis.

"Hey, what's up? No, I wasn't laughing at you, just something someone else was saying," Gloria explained, wishing Juicy wasn't in the car right now, and hoping Lamoto didn't ask who she was with. Lamoto was still pissed at Juicy.

"I wanted to do...say dinner tonight, are you available?"

Gloria thought for a minute. JC would be a real inconvenience when it came to this and she wasn't ready to bring him in on her real business. She didn't know him all that well and Lamoto would have to sign off on anyone being brought in. "Yes, I can do dinner."

"My plane should be landing in an hour and I'll be bringing a date. A very special friend of mine. You feel free to bring someone, too. We'll dance and talk on the floor about our mutual business."

"Sounds good, text me the place and time," Gloria responded, deciding to take JC, but keep him out of the loop.

"I'll have it texted to you in a few minutes, see you tonight," Lamoto promised before ending the call.

Gloria put down the phone with a satisfied expression on her face. "Okay, I might not need you tonight after all, Juicy."

"Why? What happened? Did he leave you already, girl?"

"Girl, please. Of course not. Lamoto wants to have dinner tonight and wants me to bring a date. You know him, he is a real good judge of character, so I'll have him give me his opinion on JC and what he thinks of him."

"Lamoto? I miss that man! Why don't you take me with you?" Juicy asked, thinking of all the money Lamoto used to spend on her, that is until she busted out the window of his Lamborghini with a brick. "We can still do both in case Lamoto misjudges him!"

"Fine, we can do both, you freaky bitch!" Gloria said, laughing at her friend's hormones being in overdrive.

"You know he's still mad at you. Just because he's got money don't mean he wants to waste it on Lambo windows, because he gave another girl his number. You and him were not exclusive and you know he be fucking a dozen other women. You was tripping that night, girl."

Later that night, Gloria and JC walked into one of the three most expensive restaurants in Atlanta, Luckily, Gloria had taken JC to get his hair cut at her stylist's shop and had him fitted for a grey suit which was tailored for him on the spot. It cost extra, but that was okay with Gloria because she was extremely happy to do whatever she could for JC. Especially, since he was the best she ever had. There was a waterfall in the middle of the restaurant which separated the VIP section from the regular part of the restaurant, not that there was anything regular about it. It's a place where knowing someone important got VIP reservations or else putting reservations weeks in advance could be a hassle. However, Lamoto had a lot of pull in areas which still surprised Gloria.

It had been a long time since JC had worn a suit and when he did, it wasn't to go out to eat, it was going to someone's funeral. Gloria was showing him the better side of her life, the classy side. A side that could upgrade him to the status he wanted.

"Mr. Lamoto is expecting the two of you, please follow me," a hostess announced. She looked as if she could be a full-time model. Her dress was a low cut, black cocktail dress, with stiletto heels, and a red sash going across her waist.

CHAPTER 6

$\mathcal{T}$he restaurant was a palace of marble, with grand pillars that made it look like Rome. JC placed his hand on the small of Gloria's back as they walked over to the table the hostess led them to. Gloria was wearing a teal colored dress that scraped the marble floor as she glided across. The gown was strapless and backless. A design that showcased the diamond necklace that hung from her graceful neck. The diamonds didn't stop there, they elegantly dangled from her ears with two carat tear drops, dripping from her lobes, and a tennis bracelet that covered her left wrist. Gloria made sure that JC had a little bling himself. He wore onyx cuff links and a Cartier watch from the jewelry shop next to one of her Coffee Shops. She wanted JC to give off a good first impression.

The VIP tables were made to look like cabanas at the beach. Crisp white cloth hung over the tables, offering privacy from the other side of the restaurant. There was a mini-orchestra in front of a dark, and polished wood dance floor, with violins, cellos, and flutes that were playing classical music. JC walked into the tent and sat next to Lamoto's girl, while Gloria kissed

Lamoto on the cheek as he was rising to get up and greet her. Although Lamoto politely shook his hand, JC was sure that he had seen Lamoto somewhere before. In his business it wasn't smart to ever forget a face because you never knew if it was the face of an enemy.

Lamoto was dressed in a European style with a blue blazer, pearly white shirt, expensive dress shoes and navy slacks. He wore no jewelry other than a gold bracelet on his wrist. Lamoto introduced his date as Maria, a twenty-something year old woman who looked Italian with her long, flowing black hair. She wore an elegant dress, with emeralds sparking from her neck and ear lobes. When she rose to greet the two of them, a side slit flared open on her gown, flashing black stockings and creamy thighs where her garter started.

Through the dinner conversation, JC learned that Maria was 27 years old and was an international model. She had been on a photo shoot in the Riviera when Lamoto spotted her. It was clear that he was several years older than her, probably in his mid to late 50's, but as with many older men, he tried to hold onto his youth with beautiful young woman who didn't mind selling their morals for a chance to be spoiled.

"JC, you don't mind if I take your beautiful date for a spin on the dance floor, do you?" Without waiting for permission, Lamoto held his hand out to Gloria, who accepted. On the way out Lamoto added, "Order anything you want or need. I'll be back soon, Maria. Ciao!" he said, blowing a kiss at her.

"You're not from around here, are you?" Maria asked when they left, as she fired up a cigarette.

"Nah, nope, I mean, no. How did you come up with that?" JC asked. He was definitely out of his element, and wanted to believe others hadn't noticed it, but clearly, she had.

"I can tell, you're like a mule at the Kentucky Derby," she said, laughing at him. Her voice innocent, yet sarcastic. She was probably one of the most beautiful woman that JC had ever seen. So beautiful that he found her even more intimidating than the restaurant.

"Wow. Is that good or bad?"

"I am not sure yet, could be very good or very, very bad. Please don't think what I say is an insult, I was just trying to point out that you do not fit in with these fools who walk around like they have a stick up their ass," she said, sliding her foot between JC's legs.

"Who! Wait! Chill Maria!" JC said, pushing her foot away and almost spilling his champagne on his new suit.

"Calm down before someone hears you," she instructed, pressing her feet hard against his dick. "Someone doesn't want me to stop," she said commenting on his hardness.

"What the hell are you doing? Aren't you with Lamoto?" he asked, looking around to see if anyone saw what had just happened. Thank God for the tent that covered some of their view from others.

"Of course I'm with Lamoto, but I am also a young girl with too much energy, and let's just say Lamoto cannot keep up with me on any day. He cannot handle me like I need to be handled. Am I supposed to not be satisfied? I want someone to ravish me, not parade me around like a trophy in his hunting lodge so his Republican friends can ooh and ahh over me. Besides, Lamoto changes girls like you probably change shoes. I'm just along for the ride, but that doesn't mean I have to stay on the old rides."

"Hell nah, Maria! Get your feet off of me. I'm not playing this game. You could be setting me up."

31

"Setting you up? For what? To have Lamoto kill you? Mmmm, I just want a little of what you have inside your pants," Maria purred like a crazed lioness.

Gloria and Lamoto were busy dancing as the music livened up, probably at his request. They began dancing as if they were on a date with each other, two old lovers comfortable with each other's bodies. "How long have you known that man, my dear?" I have seen him before, and I do not think it was on a good note either. I will have to do a little research on him when I get home," Lamoto added almost as an afterthought.

"Don't be silly," Gloria said smiling up at him, thinking he was teasing her. "He's not from around here and I've only known him a short time. What do you think?" Gloria asked, beaming about her man.

"I don't like him. He seems...sneaky. Like he's hiding something or from someone. I don't trust him and neither should you!"

"Seriously?" Gloria was shocked. She never anticipated this kind of response. JC seemed so normal to her, but Lamoto was perhaps seeing him in a different light.

CHAPTER 7

"Yes. His eyes tell me everything. He's much younger than you and yet he has been through many serious situations in his life. You do not want to be the person he's with when he faces the next situation, and there will be a next one, trust me. After tonight, leave him alone."

"What? This is crazy!" Gloria said, shaking her head from side to side, not believing what he was saying.

"This is in your best interest. I have never given you bad advice my dear and I wouldn't start in your personal life. Your happiness is tied to my business. You're beautiful, intelligent, and successful. You can have any man you want, just not this man."

"Now you sound like Juicy. She asked about you tonight. In fact, she wanted to come. Are you still mad at her?" Gloria asked, laying her head on his chest while she thought about what Lamoto had said. She wasn't sure it would be so easy to let JC go. If she didn't exactly love him yet, she loved how he made her feel. He was different than her past partners.

"No, I am not mad at her. It was only a car window, and it was not the money that made me upset. It was her temper. I cannot allow someone like her to be in my inner circle, not knowing how she is going to respond from one moment to the next. Juicy is like a wild stallion, beautiful and fun, but better kept afar."

As the music was ending, Lamoto whispered into her ear what he wanted her to do for him next. Gloria agreed, knowing that while he gave her some of the simplest things to do, it must be important. Too important to speak about on the phone. She enjoyed working for him, and the danger element kept her on her toes, sometimes she felt like a female version of James Bond.

Later that night when JC and Gloria arrived home, things were tense between the two of them. Gloria snuck side looks at him trying to see what Lamoto saw. They took separate showers and when they laid in bed that night, Gloria kept quiet and on her side of the bed.

It was clear to JC that she was in her own world. She had been that way from the moment her and Lamoto came back to the table. "What's wrong?" he asked, as he grabbed her arm and kissed her skin.

Gloria tried to gently reject him by saying, "Nothing. I'm just tired. I think that rich food upset my stomach a little."

JC could tell that she was lying and he didn't like it. He wanted to figure out what was going on. He wasn't about to let himself get hurt by another female, nor did he want Lamoto hating on his play if he recognized JC as much as JC did him. He figured Lamoto must have said something to her. He needed to figure out where he knew Lamoto from before something bad happened. Maria had insisted on giving him her number and he

WOMEN LIE MEN LIE - PART 3

was more than ready to use it once Gloria fell asleep. Maria had mentioned that Lamoto was dropping her off tonight at her place because he was flying out of the country first thing in the morning. JC needed answers, so he got out of bed and swiped Gloria's car keys off the dresser and drove to the nearest pay phone. He didn't dare use Gloria's cell phone to call. JC had no clue where Gloria lived or where he was going, so he jotted down her address so he could GPS his way back home. It was after one in the morning when Maria answered the phone.

"Hello?" Her sweet voice asked on the other end.

"Maria, this is JC. What up? You still with Lamoto?"

"No, he's gone. Whose number are you calling me from?"

"It's a pay phone. I don't have a cell right now. I'll try to get one tomorrow or something. Can I come over or meet you somewhere? I need to talk to you about your boy, Lamoto."

"Uhmm...you can come over. Nobody is here. I told you Lamoto won't be back tonight," she replied, giving him her address.

JC put her address into the GPS and drove to her place. She stayed in a swanky, Spanish style Condo, with a red Corvette in the driveway. He flashed his lights when he pulled up and Maria opened the door wearing a pink see through gown. Underneath she wore a sexy white bra and panty set. When JC walked in, the condo smelled like strawberries and coconuts. Wood floors and white rugs met his feet as he entered then it all went black when Maria shut the door. It was so dark that JC took three steps forward and walked right into something metal that dug into his knee.

"Oww! What the fuck was that? Turn on the damn lights, Maria" He demanded, rubbing his kneecap.

35

"Give me your hand and follow me," she said, laughing as she extended her hand. A few seconds later she opened a door and he saw dozens of lit candles, the source of the fruit smells in the house. "Have a seat," she offered, pointing to a bed with dozens of pillows, while she began to dance to some slow playing music in the background.

This was clearly her sexual playground. There were bottles of lotions, creams, and sex toys that all had a specific place, all except the handcuffs attached the rail of the bed. "I'm not here for that Maria. I need to talk to you about something." He couldn't believe he had just turned down casual sex with her. She obviously dug his vibe and he would love to tear the pussy up, but Lamoto had him more than a little freaked out. Not only knowing he had seen him somewhere before, but not knowing how Gloria knew him.

"You give me what I want and I'll give you what you're searching for. This is not open for debate. You called me, remember?" she asked, sitting on his lap and began kissing his neck.

Maria was by any scoring system a hard ten and had a body like Kim Kardashian. JC was tempted to just shove his dick in her right there, but he couldn't afford for Gloria to wake-up to see that he was not only gone, but that he had jacked her ride too. She might even call the police thinking the car had been stolen. He needed to get answers to his questions, so he could get back as soon as possible. "Wait...wait. Not tonight, Maria. I don't have the time right now. My situation with Gloria is not as solid as yours is with Lamoto. I snuck out to get here and she could wake up at any moment. JC stood up and placed her on the ground as gently as he could and found a light switch to turn on. The light flooded into the room, he noticed a sex swing in the corner that he hadn't seen before and a closet filled with every costume imaginable. Maria was a very kinky girl.

"Fine, what do you want then?" she asked, pouting her lips.

"Tell me whatever you know about Lamoto. He looks familiar to me."

"You expect me to just spill the beans to you about my meal ticket? And for what? I could get killed for telling you anything. Lamoto is a very serious player and powerful man all over the world. I don't even know if I can trust you. I came onto you at dinner, gave you my number, let you into my home, and yet you have done nothing to earn my trust," she exclaimed, putting a joint into her mouth and lighting it.

"What do you want me to do? I'm not going to say shit to no one about you. Gloria is my meal ticket just as Lamoto is for you. We're the same. You're safe with me, I just need to know about Lamoto. Did he say anything to you about me?" JC asked, sitting in front of Maria and turning down her offer to take on the joint. He needed to be clear headed and definitely did not need the smell of pot on him if he got pulled over when he drove home.

Maria was silent for a few seconds, long enough for JC to move closer to her and kiss her delicious lips. After a few warm kisses, Maria replied, "He didn't say much about you. Only that you looked familiar and he was going to have some associates of his find out where he knew you from. I am not exactly sure what Lamoto does, but even with the legitimate business he has, there is a criminal side to him and those who answer to him."

"That's it? That's what you couldn't tell me?"

"Yes! Even that small amount would be seen as a betrayal by

A. ROY MILLIGAN

him. Having sex with you could be at least understood, we are not exclusive."

"Will you relay more information to me if you learn of anything else, please? I'll get a phone tomorrow and give you the number. Call me if you find out anything."

"I'm not sure if I should do that, cell phones leave traces. I guess that depends on you and your intentions for the information."

JC didn't know if he could trust her, maybe she was a set-up by Lamoto to find out who he was. In order to solidify their partnership, JC knew he had to have sex with her to make her seal their new partnership, even though, he knew he was risking everything to do so. "How long have you known Lamoto?"

CHAPTER 8

"*I* met him about six months ago. The photo shoot was at his home in southern France. It's not like he confides in me with his business matters."

They talked for another hour about Lamoto. An hour that got him nothing in the way of substantial information, but at least she was becoming more comfortable with him. Against his better judgment, JC gave into Maria's advances, going in raw and praying she didn't have anything. He knew Gloria would have him checked again eventually. But with no condom in sight, he slid her panties off and slipped past her clean shaven pussy. Her smallish breasts had hard nipples that ached for his mouth, and she gasped when he slid his length in, pounding past what she was probably used to with Lamoto. Unlike Gloria, Maria had rhythm and locked her legs around him and matched his thrusts until she came minutes later. A climax that was preceded by moans. After they were done, JC hurried up and cleaned his body off as fast as he could with Maria trying to coax him into another session like a bitch in heat. However, he only had one thing in mind, not messing things up with Gloria so soon in their relationship. He made it home at close to four in the morning and Gloria was still sleeping when he slid in next to her as quietly as he could and fell asleep, vowing to not take another chance like that again. He wondered if she had awoken some time during the night. JC would have to find a good excuse in the morning, if confronted.

When the sun came up, JC was still knocked out while Gloria was up and about. Surprisingly, cheerful after last night's conversation with Lamoto. As she was putting on her shoes, Lamoto's number popped up on her vibrating phone.

"Hello, and good morning," Gloria said, picking up and walking out into the living room.

"Am I disturbing you, my dear?"

"Not at all. I was just getting dressed and about to leave."

"Is JC there with you?"

"Of course he is. Why?"

"Is he right by you?"

"He's asleep in the bedroom and I'm in another room, why? This is getting weird Lamoto. He's not even from here, now what is going on?"

"I don't know yet. I'm still trying to put the pieces together. But I do need you to do me a favor."

"Of course. What do you need me to do?"

"I need to know if he has any bullet wounds on his upper body. Do you know what a bullet wound looks like?"

Gloria couldn't remember if he had any or not, which is strange because she saw him with his shirt off over a dozen times, but perhaps her vision was preoccupied with his muscles and rock hard abs that defined his body. "I think I do. I can't say if he does or doesn't. I would have to check," she replied, thinking it wouldn't be too hard to find out.

"Gloria, I know I am putting you in a difficult situation, but I'm afraid I do need an answer as soon as possible. If there were another way, another person, I would make this request of them. Trust me when I say the future of our organization may rest in your answer," Lamoto said mysteriously.

"Okay, Lamoto. I will get back to you as soon as I can," she answered before hanging up the phone. She didn't know what was going on, but she also knew that Lamoto wasn't one to get wrapped up in drama or hysterics over nothing. She wanted to know who JC was and what he had been through.

"JC, wake up!" she demanded, pushing on his shoulder.

"Why you waking me up girl?" he asked, rolling over to face her.

"I'm about to leave, you need anything before I go or to bring back?"

"Nah, I don't need anything," he said rudely, as he rolled over and went back to sleep.

A little pissed at his dismissal she left and figured she would talk to him later on. She had other things to do right now, along with money to pick up. Lamoto's situation would have to wait.

A few hours later, JC woke up and took a shower before calling Gloria to see when she was coming home.

"Hello?"

CHAPTER 9

"Where you at Ms?"

"Out and about. Why, what's up?"

"I need to get a cell phone. When you coming back? You never cook for a nigga, what's up with that?"

Gloria laughed at the thought of domestication, "I don't cook much, never have. So if you have visions of a southern belle cooking grits and shit, you got the wrong girl. I have a Mercedes in the garage, grab the keys out of the kitchen drawer by the sink. Go do what you gotta do and I'll be back in about two hours."

"You know I ain't got my license and I have no idea where to go. I'll get stopped for sure in this town. I'll drive at night when the traffic's lighter."

"Well, you'll have to wait until I get there."

"Fuck it, I'll get it myself."

"No, I'll have someone come get you and drive you around."

"Who you gonna get? I'm not about to just ride around with anyone."

"Shut up and stop being so damn paranoid. She's cool. I'll call you back in a minute." Gloria hung up and called Juicy. She didn't answer at first, but a few minutes later she hit Gloria back up.

"What's up girl," Juicy asked, a little out of breath.

"What are you doing right now? You real busy?"

"I'm just finishing up a class. Why? What's up?"

"Remember what we talked about? Are you off your period?"

Laughing, Juicy said, "Yeah, girl! Damn! You sound like a man all in heat."

"Sorry! I'm like two hours away, but I'm heading back. I left JC at the house and he needs to run some errands, but he ain't got no license yet. You think you can go over there, take him to do what he needs to do, then put some moves on him to see if he goes for you?"

"Oh my God! You are serious about this. Girl, I thought you was just playing. If you don't trust him, you don't need to be around him or with him."

"I do...I do trust him. A little bit at least. Can you please just do this for me? Please?"

Juicy laughed at her friend's attempt to persuade her into helping her. "This is going to cost you, especially if I have to have sex with him. I'm not fucking no one for free Gloria. You know that. I have to take a shower too."

Gloria laughed at Juicy's comments. She loved her, even if she was wild at times. Juicy was a well-known freak around Atlanta and not a cheap one. When she hooked up with a guy, he better have gifts coming. She was not ashamed to keep her bank account fat. "Fine, you get a shopping trip at the Prada Store. Happy?"

"Okay, but it won't be a fast shopping trip girl!" Juicy promised, as she envisioned new clothes fitting inside her walk-in closet that was the size of a room.

"You got it. Now take a shower and get over to my house. I can make it three hours away instead of two, I'm getting a little hungry anyway. Call me later when you're not with him. You know I want details bitch!" Gloria said, hanging up. She called JC back and gave him her new arrival time and told him that her friend Juicy was on the way to get him and she'd call him back later.

CHAPTER 10

*K*elly arrived at her house to speak with Merido face to face. She was still in shock with what he told her on the phone, and she needed to know how accurate his information was. She sat down and talked to her mom in the living room for a couple of minutes, trying to wrap her head around it all, then she sat across from Merido at the dining room table after watching her mother go into the garden.

"So what's going on?" she asked, sitting down in the chair, not trusting her legs to stand on at the moment.

"First let me say, I don't know one hundred percent of everything, yet. My brother Lamoto has a spot down in Atlanta and he says he met a JC that looks very similar to the JC in the pictures we've been circulating. But he's not sure and wanted to get some kind of confirmation to verify it."

"In Atlanta? JC doesn't know anyone in Atlanta. So why would he be down there?" Kelly asked with a skeptical expression on her face while her eyebrows pinched together in disbelief.

"If it's our JC, he's down there with a girl named Gloria. She also happens to be one of Lamoto's top money traffickers."

"I don't know a Gloria. What, is he with her or something?"

"That's what it sounds like, but Lamoto assured me she does not know where he came from, so she cannot be aware of his past. I'm waiting to hear back from Lamoto. He promised to get to the bottom of this."

"I doubt it's him it would be too crazy that he has run into your brother's arms. We couldn't get that lucky, could we?"

"I was wondering the same thing, but you never know Kelly. Fate is a bitch!"

"True! You know I'll be waiting for your call. You give me the word, and I'm ready to catch the first flight," Kelly promised, hoping it would be JC.

"I'm with you, you're not alone on any of this. I was thinking of taking your mom with us, just a quick getaway trip. Something of a celebration. We can stay for a couple of weeks. You need some partying in your system to balance out the hate."

"I have good reason to carry this hate, so don't you dare act like I'm crazy for feeling the way I do, not you Merido. It would be good to go away though, it's been awhile since I've really been out."

"No one is saying you don't have a right to be angry, but you have been living and breathing this hatred for way too long now Kelly. It's good to let go. For you, you have two choices of how to let go of JC. I want you to think about this, don't just respond out of anger. Do you want JC killed or send him to prison for the rest of his life? I know the decision seems obvious. Just kill him, you might be thinking, but imagine this: if he goes to jail, with the murders, he'll never get out again.

He will suffer every day in there, let the prison walls suffocate him, maybe pay to have some people keep his life complicated. If we kill him, we can torture him, make him scream, peel the flesh from his rotten bones, but it will not last as long as prison. It's your call Kelly. What do you want to do?"

"I have thought about this every night before I go to sleep. I dream of the moment I look him in the eye, and not once has that dream been of watching him get handcuffed and hauled away to prison. I don't want him to breathe anywhere again. I'm not going to give the luxury of going to prison and be able to sleep at night. Maybe prison would make him suffer, but I will still know he's alive. I will still hear his heart beat every night when I go to sleep. I want him dead! D-E-A-D...dead. No one and I mean no one is to kill him. You tell Lamoto that he is to be untouched, use drugs, a dart, sleeper hold, or whatever else we have at our disposal to capture him and hold him until I get there."

"What if we send him to jail and let him do about ten years first, then I'll have him stabbed to death, maybe have his skin boiled off him, or something like that?"

"Right now, Merido, I only know that I want him captured and held. Your idea sounds painful, but I need to think about it. Right now, he is not in our hands and we don't know that this is Lamoto's JC, so let me think about it, okay?"

"Well you better think fast because that call could come any minute."

"It's probably not even him. How could he be so sure?"

"He ate dinner with him. He actually sat across from him, shook his hand, held a conversation."

"What did he say his name was?"

"Who?"

"JC, what name did he use?"

"JC!"

"We don't know enough yet, so I'll wait for your phone call. Just make sure that it's him!"

When Lamoto landed at Orly airport in Southeast France, he called Maria. He needed to ask her some questions. Gloria was taking an unusual amount of time to get him his answers making him think she was compromised at least in some way, if only by the heart.

"Hello?"

"Bon Jour, Cherie!"

"Hi, baby! You landed safely, how was the flight?" Maria asked.

"It was fine, I slept through most of it. I decided to have some shoes made just for you while I'm here. They will be 100% original, not one other woman in the world will wear these shoes," Lamoto promised her.

"That's why I love you, Lamoto. You always know the way into my heart."

"I love you as well. I was also thinking that when I get back we can go to Europe. Just the two of us, spend like a week and relax."

"That sounds romantic. I'll need to go shopping for a fabulous wardrobe."

"Of course, it would require new clothes. On another note, have you talked to JC yet?"

"Not yet. I will though. I think we have him completely fooled," Maria explained.

"I should have killed that fucker when I had the chance."

"Don't worry, we'll get him eventually. No one can hide forever."

"I know, next time. At some point though, there won't be a next time. If it's him, we have to move fast before he slips away again. I need you to get him naked or at least get his shirt off and see if he has at least one bullet wound on his upper body."

"Okay, I'll make sure to check. Why didn't you tell me that the first time?"

"Because I didn't know until I talked to my brother. Plus, I wanted to lock him in so we could keep tabs on him. As hot as you are, what man wouldn't fall for you?"

"You are a sweet, sweet man, Lamoto, thank you."

"No, thank you baby. Make sure you become his best friend in Atlanta. Take him out if you want, show him a good time, whatever it takes to get his shirt off."

"That is a piece of cake. Is that the only confirmation you need? You don't want me to question him a little about where he's from or what he used to do?"

"No, I don't want him scared away by questions. I don't need anything else, I'm about 98% sure it's him anyway. I'm simply being cautious, I don't want to grab the wrong person. I should have been done with him. I know it's him, it's got to be! It's too close of a match."

"I'll take care of it however you want me too. I can handle it."

Lamoto laughed, sensing the end was near. "I know you can handle anything, but this is special and it must be done a certain way. You do what you're told. Suck his dick if you have too."

"Lamoto, you know I don't like doing that, it's dirty!"

"Do it for me. Men love it, trust me! If you do it while he's driving he'll never forget you."

"Really?"

"Sure, why not? You better not mess this up. You got that?"

"Yes, I got it Lamoto. I heard you the first three times you told me. I won't mess it up!"

"Don't get sassy with me, Maria, just do it right!"

CHAPTER 11

*J*uicy took her time taking a shower after her pole class and wore a slinky navy dress that accented her breasts. She was about to leave when she thought about it and slipped her panties off. She wouldn't be needing them.

When she got to Gloria's place she honked the horn four times before she saw JC look out the window suspiciously. She waved her manicured hand at him to come out.

Before he got there she popped her trunk and grabbed a bottle of Armor All and began to clean her tires. She knew the dress was more like a t-shirt, but she needed to reel him in fast.

"I can help you, you don't need to get all dirty girl," JC said, walking out to the house wearing a pair of black jeans, an Atlanta Hawks Jersey, and the new Jordans that just came out.

"Oh, it's ok. I got it," Juicy said, squatting down to clean off the imaginary dirt from the tire.

JC couldn't help but notice her squatting because her pussy was showing.

I'm Juicy, Gloria told me to take care of you. Show you a little southern hospitality," she said with a smile. She let him take her hand while he twirled her around looking at the whole package.

"Damn, baby! You fine as a muthafucka!" JC said, complimenting her. He hadn't seen nothing like Juicy in a long time. Her booty was poking out so far from her back, JC thought she had ass implants. "I know that shit ain't real?"

"What ain't real?"

"That big ol' ass you got popping out!"

Juicy laughed and twerked it a little for him then asked, "You wanna feel it?"

JC didn't even take a second to think about it, he grabbed and squeezed her ass like he was testing a lemon at the super market. It was soft, but very firm like she worked out or something. She tightened up her cheeks in his hand, flexing the muscles for him. "Damn, girl! You got back!"

"I work out!" is all she said while she finished spraying the other tires.

"Where do you work out at? I need to join me a gym anyway."

"I teach pole dancing classes for the wives around Atlanta. You ready to go?"

"Yeah, I'm ready," he said, climbing into her ride. The Challenger had a new car smell, like she had just driven it off the lot before she picked him up. "You doing well, huh?"

"Why you say that?" she asked, knowing he was feeling her.

JC couldn't help but look down at her lap where her pussy was out for the whole world to see. "You gotta cover that shit up girl!"

"Cover what up? She asked, acting like she had no idea what he was talking about.

"That," he exclaimed, pointing.

"Boy, it's hot out here! Don't act like you haven't seen a pussy before. Look, number one you ain't my man to be telling me to cover up shit, and two, I'm a stripper. All of Atlanta has seen my pussy. Here, take a good look that way you won't have to keep looking at it," she said pulling her dress up and showing him the goodie bag. Her clit was pierced twice, and JC wanted to fuck her right then and there. He could imagine how good those piercings would feel against his dick. He didn't say anything as he replayed the image over and over in his head.

"You a stripper? You must make good money out here in the "A"?"

"Listen to you trying not to sound like a northerner! Yup, I make me some good money," she said confidently. She could care less what people thought about her. She was paid, and that's what mattered the most. "I love Atlanta, a girl feels free out here to do what she wants. I feel blessed. I love my life! If you don't love what you're doing, why do it?"

"True dat! Most girls where I'm from, they just looking for a nigga to take care of them."

"Yeah, you'll still find them around here, but a serious sista is gonna take care of herself first. So how did you and Gloria meet?"

"Didn't she tell you?"

"Nah, we ain't tight like that. Would I be asking if she did?" Juicy asked, making him think her and Gloria weren't best friends.

"Right! Ask her next time you see her maybe she'll tell you."

"I'm asking you, why can't you tell me? Is it a secret or something? And where are we going? I got shit to do you know?"

"Cell phone store...and I don't want to put Gloria's business out there like that. I don't even know you. You're her friend, not mine!"

Juicy smacked her lips together with attitude, "Whatever! I never said her and I were friends, I'm just doing her a favor. What you say your name is?"

"JC!"

"Jay Cee?" she asked with a deep country accent.

"Yeah, something wrong with that?"

"No, it's cute," she said, throwing a smile his way with pretty and even teeth. One of her teeth had been trimmed out in gold.

"So, your man lets you come out looking like this? Wearing no panties and shit? He asked, admiring her blonde locks and red boned skin.

"If I did have a man he wouldn't be telling me what to wear or not wear. If I don't want to wear any panties, I don't wear panties. But no, I ain't got no man right now."

JC shook his head and laughed.

"What's so funny, Mr. Giggles?"

"You! You're funny. Sounding all independent and shit."

"I get that a lot. So, what kind of phone do you want so I know where to take you?"

"I ain't got no credit or anything so you better just take me to the Boost shop."

"You don't have no credit? What the hell was Gloria thinking?"

"Damn, straight up? You just gonna judge a nigga on credit?"

"Um, yes! I do not like a nigga with fucked up credit!"

"Well good thing you don't have to like me then ain't it? That would be tragic!"

Juicy looked over at him and said, "Ugh! Shut up!"

"Do you have good credit?"

"I do have good credit, but even if I didn't my sugar thing's credit is all good!"

"Sugar thing? What the fuck is a sugar thing?"

"Sugar Daddy, boy! Stop acting all slow! You can't be that dumb? You know what that is. That must be why you all up on Gloria? Thinking she's the one!"

"I got my own money, I'm tight, girl!"

"Hmm, you sure don't like to spend it. Why did she go shopping for you if you tight?"

"Mind your business. That's my baby! I don't go asking your sugar thing why he buying shit for you when you got money, do I?"

"Ugh, you something else."

"You right, I am. But you something else, too!"

"What you mean by…" Juicy was about to say when she was cut short by her phone ringing. It was her ex, who was right behind her in his car. He wanted her to pull over so he could talk to her, so she told him to follow her a couple of miles up the road.

When they arrived at the store Juicy hurried JC out of the car. When JC went inside the store he looked back and saw a tall light skin guy with long braids walking over to the car. Juicy lowered the window and started talking to him.

It didn't take him long to see the kind of phone he wanted to buy. "Excuse me, Miss? Can I get some help over here?" He was trying to get the attention from this heavy set brown skinned woman wearing black slacks and a white lacy blouse. She looked to be in her mid-twenties. She seemed to be the only one in the store at the moment unless someone was in the back.

"Yes, what can I help you with, sugar?" she asked, waddling over to him.

"I need a good phone. Can you tell me which one of these is pretty good?"

"No problem. How much are you trying to spend?"

"A few hundred, I guess. Don't kill my pockets though."

CHAPTER 12

She laughed and showed him some affordable phones that worked well.

He picked one and paid for it in cash. "Thanks! So when are you gonna have time to show me how it works?" he asked, remembering he saw a black Range Rover outside and hoping it belonged to her.

"Teach you how it works?" she asked laughing a little while trying to figure out if he was serious. He was a hot young thing, the kind that normally didn't talk to her.

"Yeah, at least show me how some of these features work. I need to know what I'm doing. Just put your number in and I'll call you later so we can figure out together," he said, while smiling at her and handing her his phone.

She took the phone and added her number, feeling a little flustered by him now. Before he was just a customer, but now that he was close to her, she could feel the sweat running down her ass crack.

"Thanks again Amanda," he said, reading her name tag.

"Bye, have a nice day!" she said, flashing him a huge smile that hopefully read he could call her anytime.

JC walked back outside and swore it was twenty degrees hotter than when he went inside the store. The sun was baking off the asphalt. The tall guy was leaning against the car still talking to Juicy when he walked up, so he just got into the car where the air conditioner was blowing on high and waited for them to finish talking. But right at the end, the conversation took a more serious turn.

"Okay, I'll call you later and we'll talk about it," Juicy said to her ex happy that their talk had gone so well. "It's too hot and I'm not wearing any shoes," she explained, hoping he let her off with those excuses. Even though they were not presently together, Juicy had just told him there might be a future for them.

"Stop playing Juicy! It is too hot out here, and you making me wait ain't making it any cooler," he told her as he went to open her door.

Juicy tried to close the door but he overpowered her, trying to pull her from the driver's seat. "Stop, Jason!" she shouted, as he dragged her almost out. JC looked over and saw how she was fighting to not to get out of the car, especially with him yanking on her. She clenched onto the steering wheel with a death grip, but Jason grabbed her legs, which is when he saw that she wasn't wearing any panties and had her pussy hanging all out.

"You nasty bitch! You fucking this nigga? Why ain't you got any panties on bitch?" he asked, while his face turned a hellish red.

"Stop it Jason! Let me go!" she pleaded, while trying to get away from him, but by now she was all the way out of the car.

JC saw the door slam shut then Jason threw Juicy up against the car.

Damn, he thought to himself. He didn't want to get involved in this petty ass shit, but if he didn't squash it, someone was gonna call the cops. "Come on, man! Chill out!" JC said, walking around the car and grabbing Juicy from him.

"Get in the car Juicy," he told her, while pushing Jason out of the way so she could open the door. "She'll holla at you later my nigga!" JC told him.

"Who the fuck is you nigga?" Jason asked, while he swung at JC. JC ducked and hit him with three combinations that dropped his big ass to the ground. He tried to pull himself back up, but JC clocked him again, leaving him on the hot ass pavement holding his jaw. "I should stomp yo bitch ass out. We ain't even together, she's doing me a favor by giving me a ride. You stupid mutha fucka!"

"JC, let's go! Fuck that nigga!" Juicy yelled pulling the car out so JC could get in the passenger seat. He jumped in and they drove away. They stayed silent, each of them for their own reasons, for a minute, Juicy's dress was nearly ripped off her, hanging on by a lonely shoulder strap, with her titties damn near out. "I need to stop at my house for some clothes I can't drive with nothing on. I'm sorry, I didn't expect him to act like that," Juicy explained, looking over at JC trying to gauge his mood.

"Don't worry about it. If he would have whooped my ass then it would have been a good time to apologize."

"You did whoop his ass good though! Thank you."

"Who the hell was that anyway? You said you didn't have no man?"

"That's my ex-boyfriend, Jason. I like light skinned guys like him, but not assholes!" she added, still a little shook up, which was evident by her hands that were shaking on the steering wheel.

JC noticed her hands and knew that she was scared. "I wouldn't expect that you liked the light skinned type at all. Especially being that you're red boned yourself. I figured you'd go darker."

"Nope! Sorry to disappoint you, but I'm a vanilla kind of girl!"

They both laughed at that statement, more out of relief that it was over than finding it funny. "Well I guess that leaves me out, huh? Damn, I'm bleeding, you got any napkins?" JC asked looking at his raw knuckles.

"Look in the glove compartment, there might be some in there."

JC looked and didn't find any. "There ain't shit in here."

"Here, rip a piece of my dress, it's ruined anyway," she told him, pulling her dress towards him.

"You sure?" he asked, not wanting to make her anymore naked than she was.

"Yeah, it's torn already! I'd rather you get blood on my dress than all over my seats. I don't know what you got boy!"

"It's like that? Whatever! I ain't got shit, I just went to the clinic!"

She laughed and said, "Yeah, Gloria told me. She's afraid to death of catching something."

JC ripped a small piece off which revealed more of her thigh. He could really see her pussy now. She had it trimmed more than he thought.

WOMEN LIE MEN LIE - PART 3

Originally, he thought she was a hairy beast down there, but it was just one strip of hair, like a Mohawk. JC wrapped his hand and saw it was already swelling up. He hoped he didn't break anything. "We'll be at my place in a minute and I'll get you some ice and bandages," she said, looking down at his mangled up hands that defended her so admirably.

When they got to Juicy's apartment, JC couldn't help but be impressed. "Damn, this your spot?" JC asked admiring the décor that was really funky, but cool. She had a thing for seventies funk he saw. The rooms were separated by beaded curtains, a lava lamp sat on top of a headless male statue with quite a dick on him. A bean bag chair sat in the corner underneath a reading lamp and next to a book case with hundreds of books. The sofa was a retro red color, with a scooped yellow chair straight out of 'The Jetsons'. The walls were tan and cream, with hard wood floors and huge Indian rugs with trippy designs on them.

"Yeah? You like it? Most people can't dig the vibes, but it's so relaxing when I come home from work."

"This is straight as hell. How much something like this cost?" he asked, looking at some of the books that were in her bookcases. They ranged from finance, to romance, and history.

"Okay, now you just being nosy. I can't be telling you all my business. Sit down at the table while I get you some ice and bandages." She ordered him, while she went into a room that he assumed was the kitchen.

JC sat at a hand carved wooden table and unwrapped his hand. Juicy came back with a glass of whiskey, a small first aid box, and a bowl of ice cubes.

"Here, let me see your hand," she said, sitting across from him and began pouring on the abrasions. He had cut it pretty badly, probably on Jason's teeth he thought as he slung back

61

the glass of whiskey, providing him with a much needed pain reliever. Juicy took a damp rag and dabbed it, until the blood was cleared away enough that she could put a bandage over it.

While she was tending to him, JC looked down, seeing her beauty for the first time.

"Now, hold the ice on it until some of the swelling goes down," she told him, still holding his hand and applying the ice. She looked into his eyes and wondered what he was thinking. She usually had a decent read on men, but his stare was so blank it could be anything running through his mind. "Thanks again, JC. I really appreciate what you did for me, it's more than most strangers would do."

JC looked back into her eyes, then dropped his glance to her pussy. "You're welcome," he said, pulling her towards him and kissing her full lips, cheek, and neck.

CHAPTER 13

*S*he made no effort to resist him. After all, this is what Gloria wanted, why would she stop and ruin her shopping trip. He kissed and licked on her neck and ears like she was his personal everlasting ice cream cone, while she climbed up and straddled him. JC was so turned on that his dick was bulging through his pants. He knew better than to kiss a girl in her mouth, it was too intimate, but he didn't care because she was so damn sexy and he was aching to get inside her. She rubbed his bald head while he kissed and sucked her breasts and nipples. "Oh yes, baby!" she whispered into his ear, urging him on, wishing he would hurry, but never stop if that made sense in her passion riddled mind. JC stood up with her in his hands and wiggled out of his pants and boxers until Juicy could feel his dick poking at her. As soon as she felt it, she reached down and slid it inside her oozing hole. He pumped only six times before he was leaking like she was.

"Damn, Juicy," he whispered, still shooting his lava into her. He gripped her tightly and carried her over to the bean bag and began to slowly drive into her like a piston rod, and kissed her neck again.

"You like that, baby? You feel so good inside me. Perfect." She claimed, kissing his neck as he had done hers.

"Hell yeah. I need to be fucking with you all the time," he exclaimed, kissing her deeply. "This pussy fire."

She laughed while playfully hitting him on the shoulder, "You so funny! But you made me hot so quickly."

"I'm serious, I gotta hit this shit again," he said, rocking all the way into her.

"Hmm, but what are you gonna do about Gloria?" Juicy asked, leaning back into the bag so that he penetrated all of her. His strokes got faster.

"Shit, Im'a do me. What are you gonna do about her?" he asked, hitting her harder so she was gasping for breath before she came again, seconds before he did too.

"I don't know. I'm gonna have to think hard about that. I don't like a guy to be with two girls, especially if I'm one of them," Juicy told him, pushing him away so she could get cleaned up. She felt his cum dripping down the inside of her leg.

JC followed her into the bathroom and watched her get into the shower with the curtain open. His dick that had been going soft now went hard again at seeing her touch herself. He took all of his clothes off and stepped into the shower with her. Juicy turned her back to him and bent forward allowing him instant access to her fiery hole. He rammed into her full length, enjoying each time she gasped at his dick's power. It took him longer to orgasm this time, but it was no less fulfilling than the first two times.

After they finished showering, they laid in Juicy's waterbed, and talked more about Gloria. Even though Juicy had to admit that she loved his dick and loved how she made him feel, she debated whether she should tell Gloria or not. Good dick like this was hard to find and she knew Jason wouldn't be coming around. His beaten pride wouldn't allow him to. JC had a good dick between his legs and he protected her, she rationalized inside her head, trying to think of a way to keep him. At the same time, he was thinking of a way to keep her too.

"So when can I see you again?" JC asked, wondering how much she made as a stripper as Juicy drove him back to Gloria's house.

Without telling him, she wondered how she could meet up with him as well. Her initial thoughts of it being a hit and run had already evaporated from her mind. She had just come across perhaps the best sex of her life and she didn't want to give that up. "I don' know JC. This is really touchy for me."

"Well, can I at least call you or something?" he asked, thinking she was going to tell Gloria.

"I don't know," she said, in frustration.

"Damn, was I that whack?" mistaking what she was feeling as anger.

"I didn't cum the last time to be honest, but it was straight," she said lying a little, not wanting him to see how much she liked his dick.

JC felt kind of bad, thinking she wasn't satisfied with him. He promised himself that if he ever got the chance again to fuck her, he was going to make sure she came twice before he came once. He was just so horny from looking at her pussy all day, he couldn't control his dick, it was practically leaking by the time he kissed her.

"Are you gonna give me your number? You ain't gonna tell on a nigga, is you?' he asked, taking her silence as he was in trouble. He thought briefly of having her stop so he could jump out. He'd deal with Gloria later after she calmed down.

Juicy shook her head no. JC was confirmation to her that niggas wasn't shit. "What would I tell? That I fucked the shit outta you?"

"You right, you did throw that shit on a nigga!"

When they arrived at Gloria's house, she was waiting outside and next to her was a bat. "What the fuck is she doing with that bat?" JC asked, ready to leap out.

Juicy was shook up not knowing if this was part of the plan or if Gloria had gone off the deep end thinking JC had failed the test. "Uhhmm, I don't know what's going on! I just got here too, remember?"

JC looked at Juicy wondering if she had texted her or something, but she seemed equally as surprised.

As soon as the car came to a complete stop, Gloria snatched the door open on the passenger side and tried to pull JC out of the car. "Where the fuck you been with my best friend?"

Juicy tried to get Gloria's attention so she could read her lips, but Gloria wasn't paying her no mind. She was busy trying to bust open JC's head with the softball bat.

CHAPTER 14

"Chill out girl! What the fuck is wrong with you? What do you mean best friend? She told me she was just doing you a favor. I didn't do shit Gloria!"

"You dirty...mutha...fucker! I...knew...it!" she said with each breathless swing that slightly missed him.

"Gloria! Stop it! Nothing happened between the two of us," Juicy yelled out, chasing Gloria while she was swinging at JC, hoping Gloria's wild back swing wouldn't take her out as well.

"I just talked to Jason and he told me everything! Don't lie to me!" she screamed at them acting like a crazed woman.

"What are you talking about? Stop!" Juicy yelled, finally grabbing the bat from Gloria. "What did Jason tell you? That he attacked me and JC stood up for me and knocked his bitch ass down? Did he tell you that Gloria? He's pissed because he thought JC and I were together and he started pushing me around, slamming me against the car door. Then JC came to the rescue and got me back inside the car and knocked the shit out of Jason! That's why he's lying because his pride is hurt. Think about it Gloria, why would Jason come to you unless it was to get back to me. He didn't come to you before!" Juicy said, trying to make her friend see common sense.

"What did Jason tell you that's got you all riled up girl?" Juicy asked, holding the bat away from Gloria's trembling hands.

"He told me he just got into a fight with some nigga you was fucking! He said when he pulled your ass out of the car you didn't have any panties on! He's dirty! Juicy, get out of my way!" Gloria screamed, lunging at JC again.

Juicy lowered her voice so only Gloria could hear her, "Gloria wait! Stop it! Let me explain! That is not how it went and I don't know why you'd believe that trifling ass nigga anyway. First off, JC didn't do anything but stick up for me. When I came over here to pick up JC I didn't have any panties on."

JC was being cautious and smart, staying a safe distance from his enraged girlfriend's hands. "I was trying to seduce him like you asked, but he didn't fall for it. You have to calm down. Jason hit me and JC beat his ass, and that's all that happened. Me and JC didn't fuck!" Juicy claimed, loud enough to make sure JC knew what story to follow.

JC took the hint and began to walk towards her slowly, which made Gloria start to cry. She was clearly embarrassed at the show she had just put on for the whole neighborhood. JC moved over and hugged her, while Juicy gave him the thumbs up about not telling what really happened between the two of them. JC didn't even realize how much Gloria liked him until now. Even though he didn't get Juicy's number it didn't matter, he knew he had her.

"See baby, you my girl. I ain't gonna fuck you over! You got to give me more credit than that. I should go over and beat that nigga's ass just for lying on me and causing you to get upset. Juicy, where that nigga live?" JC asked, moving towards the car.

WOMEN LIE MEN LIE - PART 3

"No, boo! You don't have to do that. He ain't worth your time and he'll probably call the police on you. I know the truth now, so let's just go inside so we don't give these neighbors anymore of a show," Gloria said, grabbing JC's hand while waving goodbye to Juicy.

"We could give em' another show if you up for it?" JC said, slapping her on the ass and laughing.

"Boy, get your nasty ass in here and I'll give you a show," she said, twerking her ass while walking to the door.

Later that night around 8 p.m., JC was laying on the bed in his boxers after fucking Gloria. Although he couldn't even call it fucking with what her tired ass just did in bed, laying there like a dead person while he moved her ass around. She was thinking that she threw some hell of a pussy on him, and now she was in the shower whistling and singing, happy that her man was faithful. He knew Gloria had to get up early in the morning, but JC was ready to hit the streets and see more of Atlanta. Gloria came out of the bathroom surprised to see JC fully dressed.

"Where you going?" she asked, pouting a little, hoping she could snuggle up against him as she fell asleep.

"Meeting up with a guy I met earlier. We gonna have a few drinks at the bar and kick it!"

"Kick it? What you gonna kick it about? You don't know nothing about Atlanta and people here are different than people in Michigan."

"I ain't trying to hear all that. I'm a grown ass man, I don't need to explain to you where I'm going and I don't need your permission. That's what's wrong with you independent women, you all forgot that the man is in charge, not you! You gonna let me use the car or am I gonna walk?" JC asked halfway out the door.

Gloria was silent trying to see if she should call his bluff. Even though Juicy said they didn't fuck, she still didn't trust JC. He was a man after all and Lamoto said he was garbage. "I gotta be somewhere in the morning. Don't be all night in my car and put some gas in it too. I can't believe you just gonna hit it and quit it just like that!" In her mind, she knew she was walking a fine line. Gloria saw the bullet scars, but she didn't want to lose JC, so she held off calling Lamoto.

"Chill out and stop being so sensitive. I'll be back in a couple of hours. Like you said, I don't know shit about Atlanta, I'll probably get bored real quick. And don't be blowing my phone up all night either," he said, walking out the door. He knew him and Gloria was not going to work out. He needed to go have some fun and meet some people before she figured it out too and threw him out on his ass. The first thing he did once he started driving down the street was call Maria.

"Hello?" Maria asked sounding sexy as ever. She had one of those 1-900-call-a-hoe voices.

"What up? This JC."

"Hey! I've been waiting all day for you to call. What are you doing? You wanna hang out or your girl got you on a leash?" Maria asked, teasing him about Gloria.

"I'm grown. Don't get shit twisted. I'm on my way to pick you up, we gonna go to a strip joint. You know a classy one?"

"Strip joint? I can strip for you here," Maria said, humming some sexy music and no doubt swaying her curvaceous hips over there.

"Maybe later you can strip for me, but I wanna have some fun tonight. Do you know a spot or not?" JC asked, getting frustrated with all these bitches asking questions down here.

"Yeah, I know a place, but I'm all the fun you need, baby!"

"Get dressed, I'll be there in a minute," JC ordered her and hung up before she could say anything else. He dialed the phone again and called Amanda, the girl he met at the phone store.

"Hello?" She asked sounding unsure of answering the phone to a number she didn't know.

"I told you I was gonna call. You ready to teach me to use this phone or what?"

Amanda laughed because she was just thinking of him. But she didn't tell him that or that she had masturbated in the shower thinking about him. "You crazy! What's your name?"

"JC! You forgot about me already?" he asked sounding all hurt, playing the game.

"No, not at all. You're not from here are you? Where you from?" she asked, hoping he didn't really think she had forgotten about him and hang up.

"Why does everyone keep asking me that? Is it that obvious? I mean, I know I ain't got the cute accent you have, but I could still be from around here," JC said, trying to use a fake accent.

Amanda laughed at his attempt to sound all southern. "It ain't your voice, it's how you flirt. Guys around her don't act like you."

"Oh, you think I'm flirting, huh? When can we get together?"

"How do you know I ain't got no man?"

"If you do, he ain't treating you right, not like JC can treat

71

you. Plus you wouldn't have given me your number if you had a man."

"I only gave you my number in case you needed help with your phone, remember? That way I can impress my boss with my excellent customer service skills."

"You can serve me any time. So you got a man or what?"

"Naw, I ain't got no man! I'm single. You single?"

CHAPTER 15

"*W*ould I be calling you up if I wasn't? When can I see you though?" he asked before she answered the last part.

"Soon! I'll let you come see me pretty soon. Who is that talking in the background?" she asked thinking he was a player, chatting up some other girl.

"That's this dumb ass navigation system I have to use since I don't know Atlanta and no one wants to show me."

"I'll show you around," she said laughing at the navigation voice telling him where to go.

"Well lock my number in your phone and call me tomorrow or something, okay?"

"Okay, JC! Thanks for calling!"

"Shit, thanks for giving me your number. You was actin' kind of funny earlier."

"I was not! I just don't be giving my number out to anyone, too many weirdos out there looking to take advantage of a girl living alone," she said, smiling so hard and glad he wasn't there to see it.

JC continued running game on Amanda until he pulled up to Maria's driveway. He flashed his lights twice and she came out wearing a sleek sapphire dress that stopped short of her knees and calf high black boots. Her hair was done in a French braid, twisted around her shoulder like Angelina Jolie did as Lara Croft in "Tomb Raider." JC liked her, but he knew he could never trust this bitch, not the way she gave up Lamoto. She was too sneaky and JC wasn't about to slip up around her.

"Hey, baby!" she said when she got in the car, then giving him a hug and kiss on the cheek.

"What up? Where's the best strip joint around here? I mean expensive, where the big shots go?" JC asked her as he put the address into the navigation system. He almost put in the wrong address when Maria's hand snaked into his pants and pulled his dick out and started sucking it.

"Damn, girl. You really missed a nigga, didn't you?" he asked as her head bobbed up and down in response, sliding him into her greedy throat.

Maria was hoping he would change his mind about going to the strip club by the time she was done, but he pulled up and blew his wad just as the valet was about to open the door. She hurried and reapplied her lipstick, wiping off any cum residue that may have splashed on her face." I don't really want to go in, JC!"

"Why not? Have you ever been to this strip club?" he asked, while she shook her head no. "It's fun and I got some cash for you to throw around too!" he promised, as they got out and were escorted inside.

The club was crowded as he pressed a twenty into the hands of the bouncer and asked for a table up by the stage. There were three stages, so it wasn't like they didn't have room. The club was called, Aphrodisiac and had a purplish glow, like they were on another planet. All the girls strutted around and could easily be models, but he was sure they banked more dough dancing than they would parading their little hot asses up and down a runway. Maria hid behind him like a little girl going to a dance for the first time. JC followed a cute blonde wearing nothing but Martian antennas on her head to their table in front of a raised platform. A redhead was dancing to some techno music while stripping off what was left of a Nurses outfit, then she began giving herself an enema from a tube shoved into a bottle of champagne. Some older white guy in a dark suit wobbled up to the stage and threw a hundred dollar bill next to her. The redhead danced over to him and leaned down while he whispered into her ear. She nodded her head yes to whatever he asked and then bent forward while the freaky old guy drank the bubbly liquid directly from her asshole.

Their alien waitress came up and put a bottle of champagne at the table in a bucket of ice and gave them two shots. "The shots are on the house, but the bottles are put on a tab until you're ready to leave. Here's a menu of who and what's available for you, the price is double for you and your guest. If you need some recommendations, let me know and I'll guide you through the wildest night you'll ever have," she promised, as she came behind JC and ran her long nails down his chest.

After a couple of stiff shots, Maria leaned towards JC and yelled over the music, "I'm glad I came here with you, it's pretty cool!" She was enjoying the different shows that were going on. Not only on the stage, but cages filled with naked girls who rode up and down on them like erotic elevators. Two other girls were inside of a giant fish bowl, naked and fucking themselves with dildos under water while fish and eel slithered past them. This was clearly a no holds barred type of club. JC had never seen anything so raw and taboo.

JC waved their waitress over and whispered something into her ear. She walked away and then came back ten minutes later and told them to follow her.

"Where are we going? Are we leaving?" Maria asked, as they were led up some stairs in the back. There was a row of doors on the left and right. Their waitress stopped by an unmarked green door and said, "Have a good night," as she smiled and grabbed three one hundred dollar bills from JC's hand.

"After you, baby," JC said gallantly, as she opened the door. The first thing that came into view were two girls swinging from a rope attached to the ceiling. The room was plush with seats that were clearly molded for sexual positions. A sunken bed with black satin sheets, shelves filled with unopened dildos, vibrators, cream, and gels. An array of condoms of every size, shape, and color known to exist.

One of the girls, a dark skinned princess swung down off her swing and crawled over on her knees to Maria and slid a pink tongue into her mouth, along with an ecstasy pill. Maria looked over at JC who nodded for her to go ahead. The dressed up princess led Maria over to the bed and started kissing her while sliding her dress up and over her head. "I forgot my purse," she said while moaning, too busy with her new friend to move.

"I got you," JC said as he left the room.

When JC walked back downstairs, he spotted a familiar face drinking at the bar and chatting up a stripper wearing nothing but candy cane earrings. "Nino, what's happenin'? What the hell are you doing down here?"

Nino shook JC's hand and said, "I live out here now. What are you doing out in the open? I heard you was a wanted man. You was all over the news!"

"Man, that's a whole nother story. We'll talk about it later. Put your number into my phone and I'll hit ya up tomorrow."

After Nino did that, he handed JC his phone so he could get his number. He hadn't seen JC since he went to prison. JC made him a lot of money back in the day, even hooking Nino up with his crew. Then JC had to kill them when they proved to be disloyal. Nino wanted him dead for what he had done but wasn't about to tell him now.

"Make sure you call me, we got some catching up to do boy!" Nino told him, shaking his hand again and pulling JC in for a quick hug.

"Fasho, fasho, I'ma holla at you!" JC promised him before Nino walked away.

The lights in the club flashed down and a funky beat with some crazy bass exploded out of the speakers. JC turned around and saw Juicy being carried on stage by four male slaves on a chariot. They set her down when a whip slashed dangerously close to a slave's back. What she had on reminded him of the outfit Whitney Houston wore in the movie, "The Bodyguard" for the song she sang, Queen of the Night. Juicy grabbed a hand full of braids and grinded his head into her groin while the others groveled for her attention as they kissed her henna marked feet. This was like watching a Broadway play or something. Nino walked up behind him and said, "She's my favorite. Pay attention to this one, she's one bad bitch! Her name is Juicy," he added like he really knew her.

JC had no idea Juicy danced at this club, he never asked where she worked. But he was entranced just like the rest of the crowd. She had one of her slaves put a dildo in his mouth

77

while she rode his face, using his mouth as the base. She grabbed onto a pole that was next to her and pulled the dildo out of his mouth with her pussy and started working it in and out using nothing but her vaginal muscles. JC could see the dildo was coated with her cum, dripping all over the stage and each of the slaves licked the drippings like the dogs she made them become. The men were going crazy, surrounding the stage and throwing money at her feet. She waved one guy over who was standing in the shadows of the stage and let him pull the dildo out of her pussy with his teeth. The man was so enthralled he threw himself at her feet, begging for more in a pile of bills.

CHAPTER 16

$\mathcal{J}$C could see mostly twenties and fifties, but several C-notes intermingled. "I told you! I told you! That is one bad bitch nigga! Did you see that shit? I been trying to get with her since I been in Atlanta, but I think she be going for them girls, you know?" Nino said, still throwing money. JC caught her eye and tossed the rest of his money at her feet.

It slipped his mind that he wanted to check Maria's phone, but there was two men at the table that they had sat at earlier. He spotted their waitress and flagged her down, she nodded to the bar area as she went to deliver more drinks to the drunken horny masses. He went over to the bar and was handed the black purse that Maria had left. He was about to go into it when he saw Maria walking down the stairs looking guilty after her torrid girl on girl experience. JC looked back to see if Juicy saw him, but by then she was already off the stage and a small tittie white girl with platinum blonde hair was on the stage in a schoolgirl's uniform.

"Where did you go JC? I thought you were coming back?" she

asked, looking glassy eyed still from the ecstasy while she grabbed her purse and touched up her lipstick.

"I came down here to find your purse before one of these niggas took it, then I saw that guy over there in the leather jacket that I knew from a long time ago," JC said, nodding his head at where Nino was sitting.

"Oh! Can we go home now, I feel a little weird!"

Maria slept through most of the ride home and went straight into the bathroom when they arrived, JC could hear her throwing up from behind the door. The shots of whiskey was playing hell with her stomach. JC was pretty drunk too, but he had to see her phone. He didn't feel comfortable with her at all. He went over to the couch where she threw her bag and laid down. Going through her past text messages, he saw ones from Lamoto immediately.

From Lamoto: Make sure you're nice to him.

From Maria: Well he hasn't called all day and I don't know how to contact him. He didn't have a cell phone.

From Lamoto: Don't worry, he'll call. You're a beautiful girl. He's not going to be able to resist you.

From Maria: Thanks for the compliment, I will do my best for you.

From Lamoto: All you need to do is find out if he has gunshot wounds on his upper body.

From Maria: It's not hard to get a man out of his shirt. Be patient. Did Merido call you back yet?

. . .

JC's stomach went into knots. Maria was setting him up. She knew more than she was saying. Lamoto was using her to get close to him, but how do they know Merido?

From Lamoto: No, he hasn't called back and he likely won't until we get confirmation that he's the right JC.

From Maria: Well, I'm gonna find out tonight if he calls me.

From Lamoto: I got to go, love you!

JC scanned to some more recent messages and began reading them quickly before she came back out.

From Lamoto: Did he call yet, babe?

From Maria: I just got into the car with him. He wants to go out.

From Lamoto: Take him out, get him drunk, and get him naked.

From Maria: LOL, That's the plan, not a problem. How in the hell has Gloria not seen his chest yet?

From Lamoto: She has, but she didn't know to pay attention to that until the other day and I guess she hadn't had any sex with him in a couple of days. I think she might be compromised when it comes to him. You know how feelings get in the way sometimes. So, it's on you tonight to find out, then I can call my brother and let him come take care of his business.

JC may have been drunk, but he could comprehend the danger he was in. Gloria and Maria were against him, so why hasn't Gloria turned him in yet? They just had sex before he went out. And it was obvious that Merido and Lamoto were brothers. When he heard the bathroom door open, he tucked her phone back into her purse and stood up. "I'm tired, I gotta go," he said, walking towards the door.

"No! Wait!" she exclaimed, running over to him wearing nothing but sheer black stockings and a matching garter belt, while showering his face with sloppy ass kisses and groping his dick. "Don't you want to have hot and sweaty sex before you leave?" She asked, trying to lift his shirt up while kissing him.

He pushed the shirt down and grabbed her by the shoulders and repeated, "I gotta go!"

"Wait, please don't leave," she implored him, as she got down on her knees and pulled at the zipper.

"Stop Maria. You drunk, how about if we talk instead?"

"Talk about what?"

"About Lamoto!"

"What about him?" she asked, looking confused that he was turning down her offer of sex.

"What did he say about me?"

"Nothing yet. I already told you all that. I know he wouldn't be okay with this, us," she responded, trying to get his dick out of his pants.

"He doesn't know about us?" He asked confirming her lie.

Maria stopped what she was doing and looked him in the face as she shook her head back and forth, "No, he doesn't." Then she tried to stand up and go in for a kiss, but JC grabbed her neck and lifted her in the air. Her toes tried to reach back for the ground as she gasped for air.

"You lying ass, bitch! You think I'm stupid or something? I seen the text messages," he accused her, as his fist shot out and punched her in the stomach with his loose hand.

Maria crumpled to the ground still gasping for air while trying to get a scream out and crawl away from him. "Help! Help!" she shouted, hoarsely before two punches rained down on the back of her head. The last thing she saw was the cold tile floor in front of her before she passed out.

JC went into the garage and found some duct tape and taped her arms and legs to a heavy wooden chair. He took a rag and stuffed it into her mouth before taping it shut. When he was done, he tapped her softly four times while he called out her name until she opened her eyes. The left side of her face was already swelling up. "Are you ready to give me the answers I need?"

She nodded her head yes while trying to mumble out something. Maria knew she had underestimated him badly.

"That's a good girl. Now, I'm going to remove the tape from your mouth and if you scream, I'm going to really hurt you. I'll scar up that pretty little face of yours until no man will call you beautiful again, you got that?" JC asked her, as he caressed the side of her face.

She nodded her head once more, agreeing not to scream. She hoped he wouldn't kill her if she told him what she knew.

CHAPTER 17

*J*C ripped off the tape as hard as he could, finding pleasure in her pain as he pulled the rag out. "Now, who is Lamoto?"

"He's Merido's brother. I don't know what you did to Merido, but he's looking for you!" she answered honestly with tears streaming out of her eyes.

"And?"

"I'm supposed to have sex with you and look for gunshot wounds on your upper body. They don't know if it's you or not, because the picture Lamoto has is of a man who has long hair. They need to positively identify you before they call Merido."

"What about Gloria? How's she involved in this?"

"She's supposed to check your chest for gunshot wounds too. Lamoto is not to sure about her, he thinks she's too sweet on you to say anything."

"How did Lamoto recognize me? I've only seen him once."

"He didn't tell me, he just said he wasn't 100% sure."

"So, what does Gloria have going on with Lamoto? What do they do together?"

"She works for him."

"Doing what?" JC asked, kind of scoffing at the idea that Gloria worked for an underworld figure like Lamoto.

"Moving money for him. She transports millions of dollars in drug money each week. It gets shipped to her various shops."

"Does Lamoto live here in Atlanta?"

"Sometimes. When he does, he stays here or in his condo around the corner, but he has homes in many cities across the globe."

"Does he keep money here?" JC asked, watching her eyes for a tell-tale sign that she was lying so he could knock her ass out again.

Maria was silent for a moment, but then figured it wasn't worth getting killed over money that wasn't hers. "Yes!"

"Where? Come on, don't get quiet now."

"Behind the picture of Jesus and the disciples."

JC turned around and saw a picture of The Last Supper hanging behind him above the fireplace. "Right there?"

"Yes, pull the frame from the left side."

JC got up and pulled the picture away from the wall and sure enough a safe with an electronic keypad was behind it. "What's the combination?"

"6-34-12-9," she said, hoping to get this over with so she could call and warn Lamoto.

JC punched in the numbers and heard the lock click. It opened and there were about ten thick stacks of $100 dollar bills, a chrome pistol, and several ten-ounce gold bars with an eagle imprinted into the gold. He grabbed a bag out of the garage and came back, loading it with the money and gold while shoving the pistol into the small of his back after checking that it was loaded. "You gonna take me to his condo."

"Why? He's not there?"

"Where is he?"

"He's in Europe. Probably in Paris, or Rome."

"Perfect! I'm not looking for him anyway."

JC carried her outside and threw her into the trunk of the Bentley. He never noticed how spacious it was in there. He could easily fit two bodies in the trunk. He punched in the GPS the address that she gave him to Lamoto's condo. It really was right around the corner when he pulled up. The nearest neighbor was a half a block away, and the woods across the street made it a perfect place to hit from a thief's perspective. He opened the trunk.

"Get out and don't start acting all stupid either," JC ordered her, as he yanked her out of the trunk and set her down. He pulled out his key that she said was to the door and disarmed the alarm with the code she gave him. Luckily, she didn't play any games or else he would have been gone before any cops showed up and she'd be dead. Lamoto's condo looked like a bachelor's pad. It was all metal and glass, with pictures of him on a Safari in Africa, shaking hands with a couple previous presidents and other high profile people. He had a desk in the middle with five computer terminals, at least an "80" flat screen television on the wall, a bar with crystal decanters that probably held expensive liquors, and a humidor that kept Havana Cigars fresh. There was even a stripper pole in the dining room for his private shows. JC thought about holding her for ransom, but Lamoto was probably a businessman who knew she could be replaced easily. He searched the condo, but all he found was about $5000 in cash, a Rolex watch, and a platinum diamond bracelet. He looked for a safe like Maria had, but didn't find one. Maria claimed not to know if he had one or not. He pocketed what he found and gave up looking for anything else.

JC wanted to get out of the house because there was no telling if one of Lamoto's men kept watch over the place or if Lamoto notified local police when he would be out of town. He didn't want to be caught here. He turned to Maria, trying to decide what to do. He knew if he let her go she would call Lamoto immediately and the chase would be on. But if he killed her, he would be captured and tried. He chose the lesser of two evils and untied her. "You tell anyone anything I'ma find you and kill you. You got that?" he asked, holding her by the neck again, making sure she looked him in the eye.

Maria couldn't believe that he was letting her live, she wouldn't have if she was in his shoes. "Yes, of course. I'm not going to say anything," She promised, swallowing the lie as soon as it left her lips.

"Anything else you forgot to tell me?" JC asked, walking towards the door.

"No! I told you everything."

JC turned around and shot her six times in the chest. The first shot caught her by surprise and she looked down at the blossoming blood stain in disbelief. The next two shots propelled her backwards and she flew over the coffee table. JC shot three more times just to be sure, he wanted to leave no witness that knew him for who he really was. With a pool of blood behind him, he walked out and left the door open and drove Gloria's car down to the front gate of her neighborhood and left it there. He wanted to go kill Gloria too, but he didn't want to return to her house. She didn't give him up, which was the only reason he didn't return to kill her. He walked down the street and called Nino. With over two hundred grand, and a gym bag full of gold, he was ready to do his thing.

"Who dis?" Nino answered with lots of background noise.

"This JC, what up nigga?"

"JC, where you at, man? Come to this party I'm at, shit's off the chain."

"I'ma need a ride. Can you come get me?"

"Where you at? I'll send a freak to come get you. I know you wanna test these waters around Atlanta, nigga?"

"Shit, you know I been doing that, but send that hoe anyway." JC gave him the area he was at and in about 20 minutes, a black Mercedes with tinted windows pulled up, making JC nervous. His hand went to the small of his back for his gun as the car just sat there, then the window rolled down and he was greeted by a white girl.

"You JC?" she asked, smiling her bleached teeth at him. "Get in, don't be shy. I don't bite," she added when he didn't answer her.

JC smiled and replied, "What up doe? I ain't worried about you biting Snow White."

"Oh, you like to be bitten? Well maybe I do bite then."

"No, hell nah. No bites. You know I'm J, and you are?"

"Kathy, but I go by Kitten. That's my stage name, but I like the Snow White name you just called me."

"Oh, okay, Kitten. You gonna have to give me a piece of the action if you gonna be using my ideas."

She laughed, "Is that right? Well, we'll have to work out some kind of compensation for you. I saw you at the club tonight. I wanted to say something to you, but I seen you with your girl throwing money at everyone else but me, so I figured I wasn't your type," she added, pouting her pretty little lips.

"She wasn't my girl, she just a friend."

She was wearing a low cut white blouse and no bra that he could see underneath, a sexy yellow skirt with a slit on the side, and a light blue belt around her waist.

"Hmm, what kind of friend? Benefit friends?" Kitten asked, looking over at him, moving her eyes up and down his body like he was a piece of meat.

"Nah, nothing like that. The kind of friend I see every now and again, and probably won't see again for years. I just happened to run into her tonight. Where's this party at?" he asked, changing the subject. He'd just as soon make everyone forget they saw him with Maria tonight.

"Not far, you'll see. You not from around here, huh?"

Not wanting to divulge to anyone else where exactly he was from, JC just said, "I'm from up north, how long you known Nino?"

"Not long, I just do parties for him. I don't think I've said more than five words to Nino. He spends a lot of money at the club though, and for not a lot of return on his money," she added.

"You work with Juicy a lot?"

"Yeah, she's my girl. You know Juicy? She's at the party too. Nino be flying around her like a hummingbird."

"What the hell does that mean?" JC asked all confused with the hummingbird thing.

"That's just a southern way of saying he likes her regardless if she likes him back," Kitten explained, laughing.

"I saw Juicy at the club tonight dancing. She was shutting that shit down!"

"She always do. I'm not on that level yet, but don't get it twisted, I can pop somethin'!"

JC laughed and said, "You can pop somethin'? What can you pop?"

CHAPTER 18

itten looked at him laughing at her and stopped at the red light, she put the Mercedes in park, turned on the CD player, and got out of the car and started bouncing her booty in front of all the traffic and pedestrians moving up and down the street. They all stopped to watch the free show. Then she jumped up on the hood and the small skirt she had been wearing disappeared into nothing but a purple thong digging all up into her pussy lips. As she turned her ass to the window, giving JC a private show, cars on the green light side stopped to watch as well and began to honk in support, making JC afraid that someone was going to call the cops. JC sat there in disbelief shaking his head. *This stupid ass bitch don't even know I have this gun on me,* he thought to himself looking around for police.

Thankfully, Kitten got back inside and started laughing at the shocked expression on his face.

"Now what? Who can't pop what?" she asked, smirking at him but out of breath from the impromptu dance.

The light had turned green and thankfully she began driving again. "Okay, I liked, I like it. You got some pop, no doubt," he said. Then thought to himself, *dumb white bitch.*

"If you like that, I could teach you a thing or two. That was nothing."

JC thought about the money that was burning a hole in his pocket. It wasn't smart to go to the party with all this cash and a gym bag filled with gold bars and jewelry. "I don't know if I want to go to the party. Let's go somewhere else?"

"I have to go back to the party, but I'll drop you wherever you want me to. But I need to be at this party so I get paid."

"Who paying you, Nino?"

"Yeah, Nino and whoever else hosting this party with him."

"I'm paying you now. Let's go get a hotel room somewhere and disappear for a while. I'll call Nino right now."

He needed to lay low for a day or so, just until he figured things out.

"You gonna pay me instead? You don't even know how much I cost. You might not be able to afford me."

"I got you." JC promised, as he called Nino and squared everything away with him and told him he'd get back at him tomorrow or the next day. "Done, so we can just chill now. You know of a decent hotel with room service, pool, shit like that?"

"Yeah, I know a good place, but what you think is about to happen tonight? You still don't have any idea what my price is."

"I don't care what your price is, aint no shortage over here. How much that pussy gone cost me?"

"Now you talking. Two thousand for the night, and that's a discount," she said as she arrived at the hotel.

He watched Kitten walk ahead of him towards the room and he admired her big Coco-esque form all the way. She was a thick girl for someone with such a tiny waist. The yellow skirt accented her curves, hugging her in all the right places.

As soon as they got into the room, Kitty barely had time to drop her purse before JC was all over her like a ravenous lion about to devour its prey. He licked and sucked on her small titties through the white blouse, wetting it with his saliva. Her nipples hardened through the light fabric like she had been at a wet t-shirt contest. He carried her over to the hotel bed, ripped off the comforter and threw her onto the pile of pillows. She shimmied out of her skirt and thong, laying there naked, as her pussy glinted up at him like a pink rose.

She pulled his jeans and boxer briefs off and her eyes widened when she saw his thickness and size. He was not the first black man she had been with, but he was one of the biggest. She ran her tongue from the tip of his dick down the veiny base, sucking his hairless balls into her mouth one by one, teasing his shaft, kissing, lightly biting, and licking the chocolate ice cream cone he carried between his legs. She tested his length with caution, not wanting to embarrass herself by gagging, she twirled and swallowed him a little at a time, wetting his dick inch by delicious inch, until three quarters of him was deep into her throat. Kitten purred and absorbed those inches, breathing through her nose so that she didn't have to stop, until his body began to tense up, and his moans came into the room, he twirled her red hair into his fingers guiding her faster onto his dick until he exploded into her mouth with such force much of his cum escaped her lips and dribbled down her chin. She wasn't expecting that much to come out of him. She was a trooper though, licking and consuming every drop of his fluids wherever they laid. JC bent her over, facing the mirror so he could see her face and entered her from behind. He wanted to watch her face as he impaled her with his length. Kitten surprised him though by matching his thrust, throwing her ass into his groin, taking the very life of his dick into her moist lips. They rocked back to forth in unison for at least 20 minutes until they both orgasmed again within seconds of each other.

The next two hours passed by much the same way, one of them would lay down while the other worked them back up until they were ready to go again. Kitten had never met a man who was able to go so many times in a row. When she left that night, after claiming she had an early morning photo shoot, she was sore from the pounding he had given her. She put the hundred dollar bills he had paid her with inside her purse, but she would have paid him if he could make her cum like that everyday. She promised to call him tomorrow after putting their phone numbers into each other's phones.

JC drank some of the liquor from the mini-bar and slept until noon the next day. The only reason he woke up was because his phone was ringing. Forgetting for a minute what happened last night he answered and asked, "Hello?"

"Where the fuck are you and where's my car nigga?" Gloria asked with her voice penetrating his hung over head.

"It's outside your gate and quit yelling! What the hell's wrong with you?" He hung up without giving her a chance to respond.

His phone rang again just as he was about to close his eyes and try to fall back asleep. "God damn it! What?" he screamed into the phone.

He heard nothing on the other end and was about to hang up when a soft voice asked, "Is JC there?"

"Who dis?" he asked suspicious of anyone who would call him right now.

"This Juicy, I really need to talk to you."

"Juicy? Juicy from the strip club?" he asked raising out of bed.

"Unfortunately, yes Juicy the stripper."

"How you get this number?" he asked, reaching for his pistol in case this was a distraction for someone to kick in his door.

"It wouldn't be hard. You do mess with my girl, Gloria, and you throwing your dick all over Atlanta."

JC chuckled and asked, "What up doe?"

"I need to talk to you, like right now."

"About what? You ain't even want to give a nigga your number!"

"JC, I'm serious. I don't have time to be playin' games. Where are you? You still at the hotel?"

Now she had him trippin'. JC walked over to the door, looking through the peep hole, but he didn't see anyone outside. "What —who told you...," before he finished the question he knew right away it had to be Kitten. She was the only one who knew where he was, he never even told Nino.

"Yeah, Kitten told me where she was last night when we were at the photo shoot earlier."

"Damn, why you girls gotta be tellin' everything a nigga do and don't do? Yeah. I'm still here."

"I'm on my way, stay there until I come talk to you," she told him, hanging up before he could even agree or disagree. JC didn't have a clue as to what she could possibly want or why she was coming at him like that, but he didn't like it. Not so soon after Gloria had just called him. He was starting to feel a little nervous and wanted to leave, but something told him to hear Juicy out.

He thought back to how he murdered Maria last night and wondered if it was about that? Was he going to have to X Juicy out too? His phone rang again, it was Gloria this time.

CHAPTER 19

"*W*hat up?" he asked in a calm voice while he looked out the peep hole.

"What up? What up? Where the fuck are you? I thought you was coming back home? JC, you need to tell me what's going on. Lamoto just called me and said Maria was dead."

"Wow, really? That's fucked up."

"He said you was out with her or something last night. Can we talk in person? I don't want to be talking about this shit on the phone."

"I seen her at the club last night, but that was it."

"You didn't take her to the club?"

He laughed, "Why would I be taking her to the club? Are you serious? I aint tryna hear this shit."

"What you mean, you ain't trying to hear this shit. You started this crazy ass shit. I thought we had plans together? A future? How could you just turn on me like this?" Gloria asked, trying to hold her tears back.

A. ROY MILLIGAN

JC wanted to say a lot to her but he didn't want to start a personal war, not with Lamoto breathing down his neck.

Lamoto stepped off his private plane in Atlanta and he was pissed. He sent some people to his and Maria's place, and they reported back that it appeared to be a robbery. He climbed into a waiting limo and gave instructions to go to Gloria's house. When he got there, he walked straight in without knocking and was accompanied by two bodyguards.

"No bullshit, Gloria. I need to know everything you know about this JC guy. Do not sugar coat, give excuses or explanations!"

"I don't know much, Lamoto, I swear!"

"How did you meet him and where?"

"At a rest stop, I gave him my number, and he called a few hours later. I picked him up and drove him home to Atlanta with me," she said, realizing how lame it must sound to someone else.

"What do you mean? You just picked him up at a rest stop and drove down to Atlanta not having a fucking clue who he was or without him knowing who you were?"

"Yes! I know it sounds weird, but he said he got into a fight with his ride and they ditched him at the rest stop. I felt sorry for him. I didn't want to just leave him there."

"Gloria, I taught you better than that, didn't I? Do you have any pictures of him?"

"Yes, well, sort of. I have a side view shot of him on his Facebook page."

WOMEN LIE MEN LIE - PART 3

She showed him the picture and then he called Merido and told him to look at the picture he just sent to his e-mail. Merido then sent the picture to Kelly. They both concurred that it was their JC.

"When you picked him up, did you have my money with you? On you?"

Gloria nodded her head yes and was about to speak when Lamoto's hand reached across the table and backhanded her across her right cheek; he spit on her and yelled, "You stupid bitch! Maria is dead because of you! JC killed her, and now I have to kill you!"

No! Please, La----," was all she managed to get out before Lamoto's bullet entered her forehead, spilling her backwards into the chair. By the time she hit the floor two more bullets sank into her chest. A trail of blood from her head leaked down to an unseeing eye.

After Lamoto made sure Gloria was dead, he grabbed her cell phone and called JC's number as he walked out the door.

"Look, I done told you to quit blowing my phone up, you don't own me Gloria," JC said, when he answered the phone.

"I'm gonna rip your tongue out of your fucking head!!!" Lamoto screamed into the phone before hanging up.

Kelly didn't bother packing anything for the flight, nor did she pay attention to her appearance. She left with her hair in a ponytail, with no make-up on, and the clothes on that she wore yesterday. She got into a silver Cadillac Escalade and headed over to pick up Merido. She couldn't believe that JC was in Atlanta. What were the odds that he just dropped into their laps like this?

He could have went to almost any other major city and got away. Kelly knew that Merido had originally wanted this to be a vacation, but now that JC was on alert, it was going to be a different kind of trip. More of a cat and mouse game and she didn't want to put anyone else in danger.

Merido was waiting outside when she pulled up and threw an overnight bag into the back. "Lamoto is pissed. He wanted to go after him, but I knew he would have killed JC so he's cooling off."

Kelly drove towards a private airstrip. The pilot would file a flight plan in mid-air to save time. "I don't care if he's pissed, it's not even about him, and it's his fault that JC knows we're onto him now. He couldn't be patient, and then he went and sent in that air-headed bitch he's fucking! JC better not slip away because of Lamoto's incompetence," Kelly warned as they neared the entrance to the landing strip.

"Hey, this is my brother we're talking about. Don't forget yourself Kelly. I don't know if he's the reason JC was on to us and maybe he did get sloppy or careless, but we have all made mistakes with JC. Don't kid yourself, it's personal for all of us now."

JC was lying down and began going over everything that had transpired in the last 24 hours, especially the phone call he had just gotten from Lamoto on Gloria's phone. He was in the midst of unraveling the puzzle when there was a light tap on the door. JC grabbed his pistol and walked slowly towards the door, staying to the side in case someone decided to pump bullets into the door blindly. Through the peep-hole he saw Juicy's face looking nervously up and down the hallway. "Step back from the door and turn around slowly so I can see you," JC ordered her with his gun ready.

"Are you kidding me? Open the door JC!"

"Nah, I ain't playin' do what I said or kick rocks!"

Juicy took two steps back and turned around slowly so JC could see she had no weapons beneath the blue t-shirt with yellow lettering, a pair of faded blue jeans that were skin tight, and royal blue platform heels.

JC opened the door just wide enough so she could come in and then he slammed the door shut and snatched the blue Prada bag off her shoulder and dumped it onto the floor. Not seeing any weapons, he motioned for her to sit down at the kitchenette. "What was so important you had to come over here?"

"JC, you are trippin…I know we don't know each other very well, but— "

JC interrupted her and said, "Wait, if this is about Kitten, I don't—." Juicy cut him off and interjected just as fast.

"No, it's not about her at all," Juicy walked up to him and started kissing him with tongue. She missed him and had been craving him since the first time they had sex.

Juicy spent two weeks straight with JC, and they were having sex at least three times a day. JC had cut off his phone and he also made Juicy turn off hers.

CHAPTER 20

*I*t was early in the morning when JC heard Juicy in the bathroom throwing up. He was thinking it was all the liqour they had been consuming for the past week. "You ok?" he asked, walking into the bathroom.

Juicy waited a long three seconds before blurting out, "I'm pregnant, JC!"

"And?"

"And you the Father! What you mean, and? You the only person I've had unprotected sex within the last month and a half."

JC went and sat down on the couch, across the room from Juicy. "How you know you're pregnant?"

"Because I know. I've been pregnant before JC. I been throwing up all morning."

"So, what you gonna do about it?" JC asked her, wondering if she was trying to play him.

"What you mean, what am I gonna do about it? You just gonna drop me like that?"

"Drop you? How I know it's not one of these other niggas baby's?"

"Yeah, there might be a one in a million chance there was a hole in the condom, but you been cumming inside me the last two weeks, three and four times a day! Really JC? And if you even think abortion, that's out of the question. I'm not getting anymore of them, you hear me?"

JC took a deep breath and said, "This is not a good time Juicy."

"Why not? Because we don't know each other? Cause you too busy?"

"Yeah, because we don't know each other, but more because I'm in some trouble right now, and I don't want to put you in danger."

"What?" she asked with a confused look on her face.

"It's a long story! One I don't have time to explain right now," JC said, as he hung his head down and tried to calm his racing thoughts. Although he liked Juicy and he wanted to have a baby, it was a bit much right now. He knew Lamoto and Merido were going to be coming for him, and soon. If she really was pregnant with his baby, he had to make plans for their safety. "Who else knows you're pregnant?"

"No one, just Carren, I called her like an hour ago. Why, what's going on JC? You're starting to scare me."

"Don't worry about that right now. I'll explain everything to you soon enough, I promise. But right now I want to make sure you have this baby in peace and safety."

Juicy looked up at JC with a smile on her face. Her heart soared that he cared so much about her. She walked over to where he was and sat down on his lap, hugging him tightly, covering his lips and bald head with wet kisses.

JC was still skeptical even as she hugged him. He had been played by girls in the past, but this felt real, like when Brittany was having his baby. "If this turns out not to be my baby Juicy, I'ma kill you and the baby. Don't play with me, you hear me?" he asked, holding her chin in his hand while she looked in his eyes.

Juicy laughed, thinking he was joking with her. "Oh, it's yours. You never have to worry about that. Like I need to find a man to take care of me? Please nigga!"

JC knew she thought he was kidding, but he was dead serious. If this baby wasn't his he'd kill them both, especially after all the time and attention he planned on putting into them.

JC had been feeling her from day one, but the baby made him look at her in a whole new light. It was kind of weird because she was a stripper and all that, but he would try to make it work. "So, when I'ma move in?"

Juicy pulled away from him and said, "Aw, hell nah! You can stay right where you at, with Gloria. And you have to let me tell her in my own way and time. You think I'm gonna just let you shack up with me? Like you said, we don't know each other like that. I feel bad enough because I lied to her about us having sex, but I couldn't have her bashing in your cute little head."

"I don't care about her. I ain't fucking with Gloria no more. That bitch is crazy and sneaky. She got some serious trust issues."

"Whatever! She told me you was hitting that shit! And she had a reason to be jealous, we was fucking."

"I'm serious, I ain't never going back there."

"Well, she's my friend and I have some explaining to do to her. Regardless of what you think, she really liked you a lot."

"She didn't like me, she liked to control a nigga! You figure it out, I'ma do me!"

"You is such a cold blooded asshole!" Juicy said, slapping his chest playfully. I know you fucked Kitten, too. You bet not fuck anymore of my friends."

JC smiled, "I wouldn't do you like that. So, you gonna let me move in?"

"What'd I just tell you? I'll think about it, but I don't know you like that, not to be all up in my mix 24-7."

"So what I'm supposed to do? Stay in a hotel forever while the baby being born? Who gonna help you?"

"I have friends. Why you staying in a hotel anyway? I thought you had money? Buy a place of your own."

"I can't do that right now Juicy. I told you I'm in some trouble right now, and getting a place requires ID and I do not want my name all over Atlanta. That's part of the reason why I'm not feeling this baby thing, even though I want a baby. Anything happens to me at least I left a part of me on this planet."

"Why you talking like that? What's going to happen to you? What kind of trouble you in? I bet not find out you married JC. You tell me now!"

"I'll tell you when I'm sure I can trust you, but nah, I ain't married. I wish it was that simple, believe me."

"I'm your baby mother, if you can't trust me who can you trust?"

Later that day, they left and went to get a pregnancy test and came back to the room. Finally, they had both turned their cell phones back on and there were repeated voicemails coming through one after another.

"I knew I was going to have to do this. You want proof? Come with me?" she said, going into the bathroom and pulling two boxes of pregnancy tests out of the purse.

She pulled her jeans down and squatted, pointing her pussy at JC while pissing on one stick then the other. She finished peeing while they waited in silence for the results. In less than a minute, both test turned positive.

"Okay, I believe you," he said. Not so much shocked that she was pregnant, but that he was going to have a child. Once he found out if it was his, he could relax. He would play his part for now because Juicy had no reason to lie. "Once this baby born, I'ma get a DNA test and I don't want to hear no excuses or complaints, okay?"

"Fine, we'll do that." she walked out of the bathroom and saw two stacks of money next to the mini-bar.

"These all yours?" JC nodded his head at her as she flicked through one stack and asked, "They all hundreds?"

"Yeah, they all hundreds. Now stop being so nosey!"

"Least I know my baby good!"

"So what you gonna do for work now that you pregnant? Not stripping I hope?"

"Boy, I can keep stripping. I know you don't think you own me! I can dance until I start to show, three or four months

WOMEN LIE MEN LIE - PART 3

from now, and dancing is good exercise. Then I'll find something else."

"You got money saved up?"

"Now who's being nosey? Yeah, I got a little somethin', somethin' saved up."

"What's a little somethin', somethin'?"

"Dang, nigga! How much money you got?"

JC laughed at her tore up face and said, "don't try that reverse mumbo jumbo shit on me, I' m serious."

"I got about seventeen G's saved up."

"See, that's what we need to work together on, so things go smoother."

Juicy was about to retort when her phone rang, "We ain't done with this conversation. Hello?" She asked holding the phone to her ear. The once smiling face turned to confusion as her eyebrows closed in towards the other and her nose scrunched up, before tears leaked out of her eyes. Juicy dropped the phone and fell to her knees wailing, "Oh, my God! No! God, no!"

"Juicy, what's wrong?" he asked, as he bent down and helped her get up.

Juicy let him pull her up, but she had lost all control of her legs and sank back to the carpeted floor. "Glor..., Glo...," she stuttered out, not able to finish her sentence or breathe.

"What's wrong, talk to me, Juicy. Take a deep breath."

Juicy did as he instructed and took a few deep breaths and blurted out, "It's Gloria. She's dead! Some...one...killed her!" she manage to gasp out before collapsing into a puddle of tears.

"What?" JC asked, surprised by the news as he hugged Juicy to him and tried to calm her down. The only people who were capable of doing this was Lamoto, Merido, or Kelly. It had to be retaliation for Maria. Somehow, they felt Gloria screwed up and she paid for it with her life. Juicy continued to cry for almost an hour, then they watched the news trying to make sense of her death.

JC knew he had left his fingerprints at each house, there was no covering up his presence at the crime scenes, but hopefully Lamoto killed Gloria so his would be at both. He laid next to Juicy who was beside herself with grief. JC knew he should get out of Atlanta, his own face might be on the news next as a possible material witness in the murders. But he couldn't run from the police and Merido. One on its own was hard enough, the two of them, impossible. He wanted to kill them and be done with it. At least then he could live in some peace. It was either kill or be killed, and if they killed him, they might get Juicy too because of the baby, or they might get Juicy to get him out in the open. He didn't want that to happen, not again. He kissed Juicy on the forehead and went into the bathroom and took the SIM card from his phone, crushed it under his shoe and threw it down the toilet. With all of his connections, it would be easy for Lamoto to track him by phone. JC wished he'd thrown the phone away earlier, but he wanted to make sure he jotted down Nino's and Amanda's numbers first. There was no telling when he might have to hide again.

Juicy woke up with a startle at almost three in the morning and noticed she had fallen asleep fully clothed, usually she slept in the nude. She looked over at JC who was also still dressed and awake. "How long you been up?" she asked, swinging her legs over the edge and sitting up.

"I never went to sleep," he replied, staring at the ceiling, watching the ceiling fan make lazy circles, as he had been doing all night, listening for sounds up and down the hall.

"Why not? You have to be tired?" When he didn't answer she continued, "I have to go, it's late. I didn't mean to sleep so long."

"You about to leave me?"

"Yes, I don't want to be in the way of things. You might have plans or something."

"Juicy, its been nearly two weeks and it's almost three in the morning. If I had plans, I would be doing them or you would have already ruined them."

"I'm sorry for falling out like that before, her death just caught me by surprise," she told him, rising off the bed.

"Stay," he said, grabbing her by the arm to stop her from leaving. "I ain't ready for you to leave just yet."

"You not?" she asked, sliding back next to him, allowing him to kiss her forehead a few times.

"Naw. You got something to do?"

"I do, but it can wait. It's nothing I can do at this time of night," she said and laid in his arms until she dozed back off and slept until eight in the morning. Juicy felt like she hadn't slept at all, not with nightmares of Gloria dying in all sorts of scenarios. Each time she got killed, it started all over again. Juicy looked over and saw JC wasn't next to her. Rolling over she saw him sitting at the desk counting all the money he had and she saw the glint of something gold in a gym bag sitting at his feet partially open. She briefly wondered if he had anything to do with Gloria's death, but that was crazy she thought to herself. He had been in the room with Kitten and then her.

.

JC mentally recounted the cash, estimating in his head how much the gold was worth if he liquidated it. He had to take care of Juicy and the baby, no matter what happens to him. Of course, he wanted things to work out, but he was realistic that life wasn't a fairy tale.

"Did you even sleep boy?" Juicy asked, startling him a little. She noticed his hand went to his back. She rightly guessed he had a gun on him.

"Yeah, I slept for a minute. There's too much on my mind for a lot of sleep, plus I keep throwing up. I might be coming down with something. How about you?" he asked, smiling at her hair all matted down on one side from sleeping on it.

"Ugh, you brush your teeth?"

"You the one who needs to brush your teeth, I can smell dragon breath from way over there."

"Whatever boy! My breath don't be stankin' like that nigga," she retorted, looking for her purse. "You want to get something to eat outside this hotel for once? I'm starving."

JC wanted to say yes, but he didn't want to leave in the daytime. "Naw jus order something."

"Alright, but then I do gotta go. I have to call Gloria's family, help them if I can. They'll wonder what's going on if I don't. I'ma have to say I been out of town. They left all kind of voicemails," she said, shaking her head.

JC let her order them both something to eat and while they ate, JC asked, "So how do you feel about this whole baby thing?"

Juicy was still thinking about Gloria and why anyone would want to kill her. "I'm happy. I mean I wasn't really expecting or planning on one right now, but this is my first child. I wanted to be with the father of my children, but things happen. One of the reasons I don't want an abortion is Carren said if I have another one, there's a possibility I'll never be able to have children again, and I don't want to risk that. I was too dumb when I was young, got pregnant too young, by the wrong type of guys, so I chose abortion twice before, never again."

"Who was the father of the two abortions?"

"Jason," she replied, finishing her glass of orange juice and feeling dumb that she had clouded her life up with him for so long.

CHAPTER 21

"How did he feel about it?"

"He planned the first one for me, and the second I just didn't tell him. I already knew we was never going to work out and I didn't want a permanent tie to his life. All he cared about was selling his stupid drugs and burning through money on material shit."

"You said you wanted to be with your baby's father, right?"

"Well, yeah! That was always the plan."

"Then why don't we be together? I know we've been saying we don't know each other all that well, but we got nine months to make up for that, right?"

"JC look, I know you mean well and all, but we both know you ain't trying to settle down and you got this mysterious shit to deal with. Not to mention when you first saw me you wanted to fuck me and you was with Gloria, so I know I ain't gonna be any different that's, who you are."

"I'm different though, this is different. I'ma lay back and chill and I want to lay back with you. What I'm involved with, there

WOMEN LIE MEN LIE - PART 3

are people out there who want me dead Juicy, and for the rest
of it I ain't trying to jump around girl to girl like that. I can
fuck with you, I really like you."

"Dead? Who would want you dead? What did you do and to
who?" Juicy asked, not trying to hear all the other shit he was
laying down.

JC wasn't ready to tell her that. What if she knew what Gloria
was into and was trying to play him. They had a long way to go
before he opened up to her fully. "I told you, I'ma explain later,
what I told you is enough."

"Later? You wanted to move in with me knowing someone
wanted to kill you, but you won't tell me why? This is serious
JC! I have your baby inside me, remember? How can you be
so calm about this shit? Do they know you're here?"

"I know it's serious. I just need you to trust me when I say
things are going to be okay and I'm not going anywhere."

"It's not okay though. You need to tell me what's going on or
I'm leaving and not coming around you again."

Fuck! This girl just won't let shit go, he thought to himself.
"Someone was killed back in Michigan and they think I did it,"
JC said, dropping the bombshell on her.

Juicy just looked at him for a second with a dumbfounded
expression on her face, she didn't think it was that serious.
"They, who?"

"The Po-lice and some other people, powerful people whose
family happens to be here in Atlanta also. I came here thinking
I'd be safe, but I'm still in danger. You are too if you start
telling people I'm your baby daddy."

"Then why don't you just leave Atlanta? Run, go somewhere
else?"

"I'm tired of running Juicy. I will go somewhere else if you come with me."

Juicy looked at him debating in her head what he just asked her. She didn't know how to respond to that, "So you wanted by the police too?"

"Yeah, somethin' like that."

"How much time will you get if they catch you?"

"I'm probably never getting out. Even if they sentence me lightly, the other people will never let me leave there alive."

"Oh my God! And my dumb ass having your baby, why me?" she asked with her eyes beginning to shine with tears.

"I'm not going anywhere Juicy. Don't cry baby girl."

"Yes, you are!" she cried out. "You can't run forever JC! Everyone gets caught!"

She was right and JC knew that, but he refused to accept that he was done. "I'ma be good Juicy, just trust me."

"How JC? How? Tell me how you gonna be good?"

"I'ma change my identity, get a whole new name, social security number, and as long as I stay out of trouble and don't give them no reason to fingerprint me I'll be alright. Please, just trust me. I did it before, but my paperwork got burned up," he lied. His paperwork didn't get burned up, he just had to leave the house so fast, he wasn't able to grab it. That was when he was with his other baby mama, Brittany.

Juicy sat there shaking her head, crying silently, "This is not good JC."

"It's gonna be okay, I promise," he vowed, holding her in his arms while she cried herself out.

Later that afternoon, JC walked Juicy to her car and tried to lighten the mood by saying. "It's a shame I had to get you pregnant to get your number."

Despite the seriousness of the situation Juicy smiled and said, "Sorry about that, but things happen."

"Aw you good baby. I was just messin' with you. So when I'ma see you again?"

"Soon."

"Why don't you stop playin' and let me come home with you? You already know my situation. I'd rather give you this money instead of paying for a room, don't that make more sense?" JC asked, pushing the issue hard.

"I guess, but— "

"But what? It only makes sense to help each other out. I'm feeling you, you feeling me plus you pregnant with my baby. We need to be going home together. Just give me a chance, I fuck up, you don't have to deal wit me no more."

Juicy was listening and looking him in the eyes. He seemed sincere, but she had a hard time trusting guys because of everything she had been through in the past, especially with Jason. "Okay, I'ma give you a shot, but if you fuck me over, I'm done with your ass, baby daddy or not. And don't be giving no one my address or telephone number, I don't want your shit coming down on me and the baby. I can't even believe I'm doing this JC. Don't be running around town either, you need to lay your ass down until we figure out our next move," Juicy told him, shaking her index finger at him.

"Alright, let me go grab my money real quick," he said, running back upstairs. When he came back out she was still leaning against her Challenger. "Pop the trunk for me," he said putting the gym bag with the money inside and as he was closing it a cream colored Escalade drove up and pulled up next to them. Jason got out of the driver's seat along with three other guys wearing white beaters and saggin' jeans. They all had the same slim build as Jason, one was bald headed who got out of the back, another with a weak ass fade, and the third had longer braids than Jason did.

"You thought this shit was over bitch?" Jason asked while running up on JC and starting to swing. They went blow for blow and the other three guys jumped in.

"Stop it Jason! Oh my God, someone help!" Juicy shouted. All four of them were punching JC until he fell to the ground, then they started to kick and stomp him in the face and stomach. Finally, Juicy built up the courage to run and jump on the back of one of the guy's, "Get off of him!" she yelled biting his shoulder.

"Get off me bitch!" the guy said, slinging her off his back easily onto the trunk of her car.

There were people walking past and watching but no one helped or called the police. Finally, Jason and his crew stopped once they seen JC completely knocked out. "Dumb bitch! I knew you was fucking that nigga! You betta pray he wake back up," Jason said, laughing as he got into his truck and sped off.

Juicy ran over to where JC was and saw the blood pooling beneath him. Both his eyes were swollen and cut. His lips were busted open and he had knots and shoe marks on his head and clothes, "JC," she said softly, shaking him but getting no response. He was knocked out. Without thinking of the consequences Juicy grabbed her cell phone and called 911. She sat next to JC while the sirens wailed in the distance. When the ambulance pulled up after the police, she briefly explained what had happened. The paramedics refused to allow her to get in the ambulance, so she had no choice but to follow in her car.

JC spent two days in the hospital and had his jaw wired to heal the broken mandible. Surprisingly, the hospital released him early because of a huge traffic pile up that involved a school bus and they needed the room. The hospital released him to Juicy who had made up a fake name for him to the police. She said she didn't know why the men had jumped him and that she hadn't seen them before in her life. She gave JC a pair of dark sunglasses for his swollen eyes and she had to help him walk because of his ribs being bruised. He couldn't talk and was placed on a liquid diet. Juicy planned on taking good care of him hoping that no other drama occurred before he healed, because he was truly defenseless.

Lamoto hadn't heard anything about JC and he was becoming frustrated. He knew he killed Gloria prematurely, a fact that Kelly didn't stop reminding him of. He had put word out on the street with his connections, but so far JC had eluded them. *He might not even be in Atlanta anymore,* he thought to himself as he drove his yellow and black Lamborghini down the main street when he was pulled over by an unmarked, black SUV. "What now?" Lamoto asked out loud, as he pulled over to the shoulder. He waited as two men walked up wearing nearly identical grey suits.

"Lamoto! What's up boss man, we thought it was you."

"Nothing, what seems to be the problem?"

"You...we're going to need you to step out of the car for us," the shorter man with dark hair stated as he stared at Lamoto behind mirrored sunglasses.

"For what? Give me my ticket so I can be on my way."

"This isn't about a ticket asshole. You think we pulled you over for a fucking ticket?" the tall bald headed cop asked reaching into his back pocket for ID, "I'm Agent Mason, and that's Agent Huyniski. We have some questions for you regarding a murder, so once again, step out of the car and keep your hands where we can see them," Mason ordered Lamoto, pulling back his jacket and putting his hand on his black 9mm service pistol.

Lamoto, being arrogant, used his blue tooth and called his lawyer using the voice activated system, "The feds are taking me away in handcuffs, meet us down there," he ordered his lawyer before stepping out the car.

They placed him in handcuffs and stuffed him into the SUV, leaving the expensive car to be stolen or stripped, "We know all about you Lamoto."

"Really? I doubt that." Lamoto claimed rather smugly to these tin badges.

"You can believe what you want, but if you don't cooperate with us, we're going to take you down. I want to know who killed Gloria and Maria Santini?"

"I don't know what you're asking me for. That's your job to find out who killed these two women. Why are the Feds involved in these murders? Isn't that a little below your pay grades?'

The agents both laughed at his brazen attitude. "Listen, Lamoto, do you really think we don't know about your extracurricular activities, like smuggling in kilos of heroin? You've been importing them every month from the big boss, De lo Gonza. We know about everything you do and if you still want to get your 300 kilos that's coming in this Friday you'll tell us what we want to know," Mason said bartering with Lamoto.

"And why? Because we know, you know!" the other agent added, looking in the rearview mirror at Lamoto.

"Or... we can just bust you and your organization this Friday and make things difficult for you. Maybe Gonza forgives, but maybe he don't. 300 kilos is a lot of dope to lose, plus I can guarantee that you'll never get a piece of ass again, unless it's from one of your cell mates," Mason threatened him as they began to tag team Lamoto.

Lamoto was quiet. They had clearly been watching his organization for some time, and they knew he was the North American leader.

"I'm sure you've heard of what happens to the big boys that don't play ball with us, right? Look at Bernie, you think we didn't know about his Ponzi scheme? We let him do it because eventually he had info on a child sex ring, but he didn't play ball, thought his money could get him off and he has decades to do in the pen," Mason explained to Lamoto.

"You'll end up in prison for the rest of your life, if your boss don't have you killed," Agent Huyniski promised him.

"I'll give you the guy that killed Maria, he was trying to get at me, and when I refused to cooperate, he killed her, but I don't know where he is. If I did, we wouldn't be having this discussion, he would already be dead," Lamoto said, deciding to help them and himself at the same time.

"Name? And it better be accurate info, you won't get another chance Lamoto," Mason told him pulling out his notebook.

"He goes by the name of JC. Him and Gloria were messing around for some time. Maybe he got mad at her, maybe she found out he killed Maria. The motives are endless. I had dinner with them both a few days before Maria's death."

"Give me a description, last name or something besides JC," Mason said, as he tossed the notebook and pen to Lamoto after reaching over and uncuffing him.

"You should know who the guy is, he's wanted in Michigan for multiple murders."

"Jason Cakes? That's the JC?" Agent Huyniski asked.

"He's in Atlanta? What the hell is he doing here?" Mason asked Lamoto.

"Okay, listen. We know Gloria was working for you and that Maria was one of your little whores, but are you sure that he's the guy we should be looking for, Lamoto?" Huyniski asked him, thinking of the promotion he was going to get after this case was solved.

"I'm sure, positive. Gloria told me he asked questions about me after we had dinner. Maybe he works for a rival crew, that's for you two to solve."

"And Maria? How was she murdered? It happened in your home and we saw the text messages between the two of you on her phone. Was she not cooperating with him?"

"It had to be JC as well."

"Explain it to us on how it would make sense for him to kill a whore?"

"We went to dinner and Gloria asked me to check JC out to see if he was a good guy because the two of them were dating, but she didn't know a lot about him. I brought Maria to flirt with him while Gloria and I danced. While they were at the table he took Maria's number."

"Her real number?" Mason asked writing all this down.

"Yes, her real number," Lamoto replied.

"Why would she give him her real number?"

"Why wouldn't she? She was my girl, she saw no danger in it."

"Lamoto, don't bullshit me! I will have your ass under the jail if this is some bullshit story! Tell me the fucking real deal, you piece of shit! I know damn well your heart ain't so grand that you're going to play cupid, even if Gloria was one of your biggest money launderers!" Agent Huyniski told Lamoto.

"Alright, alright. I put her up to it because JC looked familiar to me. I remembered my brother telling me about a JC and sending me pics of a guy that looked like the person I was having dinner with, but this JC was bald, so I wasn't sure. They exchanged numbers and went out a couple of times, maybe had sex. I needed to verify his identity by finding out if he had any bullet wounds on his upper chest. JC must have found out what we were up to, got mad and killed her. Trying to send me a message, I guess," Lamoto told them, finally giving them the real story, all but him killing Gloria. If he could pin this on JC all the better. Lamoto could just as easily have him killed in prison.

"So JC is our suspect in both murders?" Agent Huyniski asked Mason and Lamoto.

"Yeah, it has to be him," Lamoto chirped in, supporting their beliefs. This was going to be easier than he thought.

CHAPTER 22

"*A*lright, we believe you. We'll take you back to your Lamborghini, if it's still there," Agent Mason said with a smile on his face, hoping someone trashed it.

They dropped Lamoto off where they picked him up, after charging him a $10,000 dollar pain in the ass fee. Lamoto was pissed at the inconvenience of having to rat to get clear and pissed that his organization had been under the eye of the Feds for a long time and none of the cops he had on the side knew anything about it. He got into his car and pushed the pedal down until it hit 100 mph all the way to his attorney's office. Calling him on the way to get back to his office when he was headed to the Fed building to get Lamoto's bond posted, but now he had to turn around.

By the time Lamoto arrived, his attorney was in the office talking to another client. "Get out! Now!" Lamoto told the older white guy with a horrible dye job to cover his grey hair. He started to protest, but Lamoto grabbed and pushed him out the door, slamming it shut behind him.

"Real smooth, Lamoto. You do know I have other clients, one which you just threw out of the office? Now what happened?" His attorney asked, going to a built-in bar and pouring Lamoto a stiff scotch, straight up. "Mary, will you tell Mr. Thompson to come back in an hour and let him know we won't be billing him for today because of the inconvenience," Alan Braxton III said into the intercom to his secretary. He poured himself a drink and took off the suit jacket that no doubt, cost three hundred dollars by itself. He lived a lavish life paid for by Lamoto, his best and most illegal client. Alan had a robust torso fed with the best food around Atlanta and a lot of it. He wore a red silk tie, beneath a charcoal suit, and black shoes that were shined until they mimicked mirrored glass.

Lamoto watched him for a few seconds and then walked over calmly and grabbed Alan by his yuppie throat and said, "Look, you fat fucker! You told me every federal agent in the state of Georgia was on the payroll and that if anything was going down about me you'd know it. You fucking liar!" Lamoto said, as he spit the word liar out of his mouth and smacked Alan four times across the face.

"They are, every one of them!" Alan claimed, as he sniffled and started to cry a little bit, as blood dripped out of his nose from one of the smacks.

"Don't you fucking sit here and lie to me. If that was the case, I wouldn't have been picked up by two Feds by the name of Mason and Huyniski, would I? You want to know what happened?" Lamoto asked, smacking him even harder this time. "I was pulled over by these two wise guys," another smack followed before he continued. "They questioned me about Maria's and Gloria's murders. And then they told me, if I didn't cooperate, they would bring the whole operation down. An operation they have been watching for a while," Lamoto said, smacking him again.

By this time, Alan Braxton III was covering himself in the corner, thinking Lamoto was going to kill him and he was pretty sure he had pissed in his pants a little.

"I don't know what to tell you Lamoto, maybe they came from another branch?"

"Then maybe, you should find out before they find you at high tide in the Gulf of Mexico, you fat fuck!" Lamoto threatened him.

Alan scrambled to his feet, eager to please Lamoto and not be slapped again. He typed in a bought password for the Georgia Federal system and came up empty. "There are no Federal Agents by that name."

"I want pictures, those fuckers are dead! Do you hear me? I want pictures of every agent by the end of the day. Hack into whatever traffic cameras they have, every employee database and find me their faces," Lamoto shouted out at him as he stormed out of the office, past Alan's assistant who came running into the office in Lamoto's wake.

When Lamoto went out to his car and calmed down, he called his brother and told him that it might be a good idea to make a move on JC right now, before he had a chance to slip through their fingers again.

Merido had a previous obligation and was flying out, but Kelly would stay behind to coordinate the search for JC.

That night, Lamoto's attorney was at his front door with a big folder of pictures from every known Federal Agent in Georgia. Lamoto went through them as Alan stayed a safe distance away in case he went crazy again. Alan had to work hard to convince his assistant not to call the cops last night about the assault. It cost him a raise, a free ride to a paralegal school, and

WOMEN LIE MEN LIE - PART 3

the promise of when she graduated, she would work for him in that capacity.

Lamoto looked at each picture carefully until he set two aside. "It was these two," he stated, pointing at the pictures of Huyniski and Mason.

"You sure?" Alan asked, picking up the two pictures.

"Yeah, I'm sure! You fucking idiot. Didn't I just pick them out?"

"Okay, okay, I'm just making sure, Lamoto."

"Find out where they live and with who. They're both dead men walking, playing games with me like that."

"The reason they're not listed in the database is because it's not their real names Lamoto. These are two of the biggest organized crime agents in the U.S. You sure they wasn't just looking for a pay off?"

"They left me. Why aren't they already paid off, is what I want to know?"

"If they aren't in the database, I can't pay them off Lamoto, but if they took money it's a good sign that they can be bought. You want me to have someone approach them?"

"No! You find out where they live, you have 24 hours Braxton!"

"I'll find out right now," Alan promised, pulling out his phone and dialing a number. He had Lamoto fax the pictures to his contact in the Fed building and within minutes, he had both their real names and addresses. He wrote it down for Lamoto and left, promising Lamoto it wouldn't happen again.

"You're lucky I don't find another fucking attorney!" Lamoto said, before slamming the door in Alan's face. Lamoto would have killed him, but he was one of the best lawyers in the south and he was motivated by money. He had to remind himself that Alan was not just an ordinary lawyer, but they both needed each other. If things worked out, Lamoto would make it up to him, perhaps season tickets to the Falcons.

It had been a while since Juicy had been at work because she was too busy taking care of JC. The only place she did go was to Gloria's funeral. It was a sad and somber affair, her friend was way too young to die. It was only because of JC needing her that she was able to cope so well with her friend's death. JC still could only mumble and all his food had to be liquefied. His jaw would need to stay wired for a few more weeks while it healed and got stronger. They hadn't even had sex because he didn't seem to be in the mood, but she was super horny, taking it upon herself to pleasure herself in the shower. She felt so bad the way things went down and she couldn't help but think it was all her fault, so she did everything in her power to, if not make him happy, make him content. It wasn't hard because he didn't want much, nor could he do much. His face was still puffy and an ugly purple color. The swelling had gone down a little, but it was clear that he had just gotten his ass kicked.

"You hungry baby?" Juicy asked him.

He shook his head no and started writing something down on a pad she gave him to communicate with. It said he was going to get Jason and asked if she knew who the other three guys were.

"Yes, I do, but baby, right now you have to get stronger, okay? Just relax for now!" Juicy was worried that he would cause more trouble. JC promised her he would be good, but going to look for Jason and his friends would only bring more problems to her doorsteps. She knew his pride was hurt, but he had enough problems right now.

As planned, Juicy continued seeing Carren about the pregnancy. She was happy to report each week to JC that everything was normal with her and the baby but Juicy noticed that each time she went to see Carren, she was acting like she was mad at her or something. So one day, when the nurse left, Juicy confronted Carren about it.

"What's the matter with you? You miss Gloria or do you have a problem with just me?"

"The only problem I have is that Gloria is dead and I hear you've been shacking up with her man. Maybe it's his baby you carrying too. Makes me wonder if you know something about her murder."

"What? Are you serious, Carren? I loved Gloria and I would never do anything to hurt her."

"I can't tell. You know JC tried to get my number when Gloria had me check him for STD'S? What makes you think he'll stay faithful to you?"

They argued back and forth, until they came to an understanding. Juicy never confirmed that JC was the father, but Carren had her suspicions. Juicy told Carren she was just helping JC out because he had been in an accident right after Gloria's murder and he didn't have anywhere to go. When Juicy went home, she told JC what had happened. JC told her not to worry about him, but he made a mental note to kill Carren, she may not know much, but he thought she knew a lot, which could be just as dangerous as putting Juicy's and the baby's life in danger.

. . .

A month later

At least the wire was removed from his jaw and he could eat again. JC was surprised by how much weight he had lost since he was beaten. His ribs had healed and now he was lifting weights, and building his strength back up. JC drove Juicy to work now that he didn't need her help. She made JC promise he wouldn't be hanging around the club, staring down men who were hounding after her and causing her to lose money.

JC kissed her goodbye and went to a coffee shop that had free wi-fi and looked up Carren's address. She was a doctor and he figured there was a high probability that she was listed and he was right. She lived in a prominent area outside of Atlanta. He watched her house, looking for signs of motion lights, and dogs that could give away his presence. JC cautiously circled her house, being careful to wear a pair of black leather gloves and ducking down when the neighborhood security drove by. He could see the telltale signs of an alarm system in place, but he looked through the windows at the top of the front door and saw she hadn't bothered to set it. Typical wealthy homeowner, thinking crime was just an urban myth that happened only in the slums. JC circled around back and used a switchblade to slip in between the window caulking to open her window lock. Once inside a room that was what looked like an office, he tiptoed to the door and listened for any sound inside. He didn't hear any noise as he eased the office door open, praying that it didn't creak to give him away. Without making a sound, he walked down the hall and randomly opened doors until he found hers on the third try. He could hear the hum of a fan blowing in the corner, blocking any noise he might have made entering her house. JC could just make out her sleeping silhouette, unaware of the danger lurking in the room. Not wanting to shoot her with the same gun that killed Maria, JC put a pillow over her face and pushed down. Carren instantly awoke and began thrashing around, almost succeeding in dislodging JC, who was weaker than he thought. He punched her through the pillow in the face area twice and held the pillow until finally she stopped moving. JC looked around and decided to make it look like a burglary and emptied her dresser drawers, dumped out her jewelry box and pocketed the more expensive stuff. He also found some prescription Oxycodone and Xanax and dumped those into an envelope and threw the pill bottles on the floor. He rummaged through her purse, removing cash and credit cards. He went back into the bedroom and saw that Carren had somehow survived his attempted choking and was crawling out of bed towards the phone. JC jumped on top of her and turned her over. He saw in her eyes the recognition of who he was. "You just had to be nosy, huh? You should of worried about yourself you dumb bitch!" he said, squeezing her neck in his hands until he felt her esophagus crack under the strain of the pressure from his hands. For good measure he ripped her baby blue nightgown to shreds, took her white panties off and shoved them into her mouth, then he inserted a pill bottle into her hairy cunt. Only when he was done, JC looked around to survey the damage he had caused. When he left the house the same way he entered, he made sure to leave the window open so they would know how the break-in happened.

Juicy heard about the murder the next day and brought it to JC's attention.

"Baby, did you watch the news?"

"Nah, what up?" JC asked.

CHAPTER 23

"*S*omeone broke into Carren's house to rob and rape her!"

"Is she okay? Do you want me to drive you to the hospital to see her?" JC asked, making a show of grabbing the keys off the table.

"No, she's dead! They killed her!" Juicy told him, breaking the news.

"Wow, that is some trippy shit baby! They catch who did it? That shit ain't right raping no woman!"

"Nope, they ain't found who did it, but they said they suspect at least two people were involved. Oh, my God! I can't believe it, I wish I wouldn't had said certain things to her."

"Hey, don't do that to yourself. Carren wouldn't want you trippin' over that shit. We need to find another doctor. Worry about our baby!" JC told her, walking up behind her and cradling her growing stomach in his hands.

"You right boo!" was all Juicy said, not having a clue that her boyfriend is technically a serial killer. She had no idea how cold blooded JC actually was.

That day after taking JC to the hospital to get his jaw checked on, they found her an obstetrician to replace Carren. Although his jaw had healed, there were still bruising underneath JC's eyes. His weight was coming back now that he was eating mostly solid foods. He still had to stay away from steak and other grisly, fatty meats, but he wasn't looking sickly like before.

Juicy was happy because even though they hadn't had sex in a while she hoped he would want to soon.

"I need to get some workout equipment in the crib so I can get back into shape," he commented on the way back from the hospital.

"Yeah, you lost some weight that's for sure, but you're still handsome boo! What you need to do is work this pussy out," she told him.

JC laughed and took the hint. He knew he'd been avoiding her attempts at sex, he didn't feel like it though. JC had no doubt that Juicy pleasured herself in the shower, he heard her vibrator humming, though he pretended not to.

"Can I please get me some dick tonight?"

JC laughed again at her boldness, something he found refreshing after sex with Gloria's stale ass.

"It's not funny! You been so mean to me. I've tried to give you head and everything and you just pushed me away. I even tried when you was sleep."

JC continued to laugh which only made Juicy keep going on about how she had been neglected. "That is not funny or normal JC. You so lucky I'm having your baby because I would've went and got me some dick!"

"Well I'm good now, I got you. I've just been feeling so weak. You see all the damn weight I've lost."

"Yeah, you looked sick, but I knew you'll gain it back."

"Where you want to get some workout equipment at?" JC asked, looking at the shops they were passing.

"Nowhere in Atlanta, I ain't trying to run into anyone I know or you know!"

"Oh, you don't want to be seen with me?"

"Boy don't even play! Hell nah I don't want to be seen wit you!"

"Shit, I don't want to be seen with your ass either!" he said, squeezing her thigh to show he was joking, but hard enough for her to stop sassing him.

"Ouch! Stop before I get into a wreck!"

"Quit talking shit then. I know I lost weight, I'm back though."

"Okay, we can go to this one mall, It's like two and half hours away though. You gonna help me drive?"

"I'll drive on the way back?"

"Deal," Juicy said, agreeing as she headed on the freeway.

They went to a mall outside of the Atlanta area that wasn't as high and bought a tread mill, and a work-out bench with 400 pounds of weight to go with it. JC also bought a pull-up and dip bar set. The salesperson who rang them up told them it would be a week before it got delivered, but JC paid in cash and a little extra for next day delivery. Then they went and purchased some clothes and shoes for him, with Juicy guiding him on what was hot right now in fashion. He liked shopping with her because even though they were only shopping for him, she was still into it. She wanted him to look good and it showed in her thoughtful taste.

While Juicy took a nap JC drove them back home, following the directions of the annoying GPS voice. Juicy would have to work tonight and she needed her rest, her and the baby. She was wearing a red sun dress and while she slept, it kept riding up her thighs showing JC her pussy. She never wore any damn panties, no wonder Jason got all pissed thinking she was fucking behind his back. Everyone could see that coochie. Juicy had proved to him that she was with him and he was beginning to trust her more. He knew she cared about him, maybe more so because of the baby she was carrying, but enough for him to relax around her. He never would have guessed he'd have a baby by a stripper, nor did he actually think he would like a stripper the way he liked her. He smiled and reached over, patting the baby through Juicy's belly light enough so Juicy didn't wake up but enough for the life inside to feel his hand.

When Juicy was at work JC was working out hard, gaining his weight back since his appetite returned, making her buy more groceries and protein. Not just for him, but Juicy worked out half the time and since he had got a treadmill, she canceled her gym membership and sweated next to him. She had converted the extra bedroom into an exercise room and gave the bedroom set away to a friend. By the end of the month JC's weight was back to 180 pounds and he was solid again.

CHAPTER 24

*J*uicy's premonition that she would be able to work for a few months proved to be wrong. Her morning sickness had gotten worst.

"Jennifer," JC yelled out to her.

"Oh, since I don't strip no more you think you can call me by my government name?"

"I was just seeing if you'd answer to it. A little test baby!"

She laughed, "It's my name, why wouldn't I answer to it, silly?"

Today, JC was going to meet up with Nino. He had to get some extra money coming in from somewhere. Him and Juicy was good, but he had never been a person who was content with just being good, he always wanted more. He kissed Juicy goodbye and promised to pick up some Vernors for her tummy aches and left in a Yukon truck he had Juicy rent. He called Nino on the way and set up to meet at a public place outside of Atlanta.

"What up, boy? How you been?" Nino asked with a big smile on his face. "Why you take so long to call me?"

JC dapped his fist and sat across the table from him at the pizza joint that claimed to have Chicago style pizza, which he doubted. "Some shit happened so I had to chill out for a minute. I got into it wit some nigga. Him and his boys jumped me and I had to get my shit wired up."

"Damn, for real! You know who it was?"

"Nah, not all of them. Just the one. I had whopped him and he came back at me and caught a nigga slippin. Them niggas got down."

"Why you ain't call me? You know I woulda had your back. When you find out who the rest of them is call me, I got nigga's that'll handle that."

"I ain't gonna feel right unless I get them myself."

Nino shook his head and smiled at him, "You ain't changed a bit. You still ain't learned that it's better at the top cause you ain't gotta get your hands dirty."

"I don't be around niggas like that. I fly solo, baby boy!"

"Listen man, whatever the problem, you holla at me, okay?"

"I'll keep that in mind."

"Look at you, you done got diesel on a nigga!"

"JC laughed, "This ain't shit, a little somethin' for the ladies."

"Oh, it's for the ladies, huh? Ok den, so what brings you to Atlanta?"

"Somethin' different is all, change of scenery. You?"

"More money, plain and simple. I got it made out here. You got your hands on anything right now?" Nino asked, biting into his second piece of pizza with extra cheese.

"Nah, not yet! What you got going on?"

Lowering his voice so the regular folks didn't overhear him, Nino claimed, "I got it all baby! Whatever you want, ya boy can get it for you!"

"I know I can move the powder. I got a few white boys up in Ohio I used to deal with. All I gotta do is call them and set it up."

"What about here? You got any clientele yet?"

"Man, I don't know anyone out here to fuck wit on that tip!"

"Listen, that Ohio shit sounds cool, but you gotta get you some business out here too. Meet a few strippers, they be knowing all the niggas getting money out here. Let me introduce you to a couple of guys. You'd be surprised by how many bricks niggas moving down here in Atlanta. This shit ain't like Michigan nigga. There's a lot of millionaires down here. Niggas eating around this bitch fo' real!"

"So what them bricks be hittin' for down here?"

"Right now, 26."

"Damn, that's straight. Them bitches going for 38, 40 in Michigan."

"Shit, if it's laying like that, stick wit them, fuck these niggas around here."

"How much you give me five bricks for? Like tomorrow?"

"You got cash money? because credit comes with a little extra."

"Yeah, I'll get the cash!"

"125, that's a steal at 25 each," Nino said, floating him a price, but already planning in his head to rob JC for the money and then killing him.

JC thought about it, finished his pizza and told Nino he would get back at him tonight with an answer. When he got home, Juicy was walking around in a tight off-white dress. "Damn! You lookin' fine tonight!" JC complimented her followed by a whistle.

"Don't try to sweet talk me, where you been?" Juicy asked with an attitude. He had been gone for a while.

"I told you I had to take care of some business. Why you trippin'?"

"What kind of business and with who?"

"Chill out Juicy," he said, moving closer to kiss her on the forehead.

"Don't kiss me, and move outta my way!"

"Why you always getting an attitude?"

"Because nigga, you supposed to be laying low and you out doing whatever. You think you slick! Let me find out!"

"Find out what? What you talking' about? Come here girl!" he commanded her while wrapping a hand around from behind and kissing her bare neck. "Stop acting like that!" he ordered then slapped her booty.

"Ouch! Stop doing that, it hurts," Juicy complained.

"Then quit with the attitude and take them damn rims off your car too."

"Why? I like my rims."

"Just because I might want to drive it instead of this rental."

"There you go, trying to control shit. It never fails with you man."

"What you mean control shit? It just makes more sense, don't you think?"

"Whatever JC. Take the damn rims off then!"

JC laughed at her and said, "You crazy Juicy. Does it make sense or not?"

"No, JC. It don't! Sorry, but I ain't feelin' you on this one," she told him, sitting down at the table and began eating the meal she had cooked for them.

JC sat down next to her and explained, "You know people are looking for me and I ain't trying to drive a car with some big ass chrome rims. Sell that shit and get some of your money back."

"I will JC, I get it," she said, taking her fork and poking at the piece of steak in front of her.

"You trying to be funny?"

"No, JC!" she told him with a smile on her face. "I get it, baby. Here taste this," she added, feeding him a piece of steak. Juicy didn't really care. Whatever JC wanted to do she was with it, unless it was some crazy stuff. She understood where he was coming from with the rims and it did make sense to her. Juicy knew that JC cared about her and he wouldn't tell her anything that was wrong. And as hard as it was for her to take his advice most of the time, she swallowed her pride and did it anyway, or at least tried it to see if he was right or wrong. "I have a bone to pick with you too."

"Shoot!" he said, shoving a piece of steak into his mouth. It was marinated with something sweet and spicy.

"Shoot? What does that mean? Is that some Michigan shit or something?"

"Shoot just mean, go, let me hear it."

"Oh, anyway, why havn't you ate my pussy?"

JC almost choked on the piece of meat he was about to swallow, "What?"

"Nigga, you heard me. Why havn't you ate my pussy? I give this pussy to you whenever you want it, how you want, and where you want it. Plus I suck your fat ass dick, but you never seem to want to return the favor."

JC was silent, wondering how he was going to explain to her why he didn't.

"I'm listening! You got all day to think."

JC smiled at her and said, "I don't know. Is that what you want me to do? I-."

Juicy interrupted his excuse and said, "Nah, you know what? I want to hear the real JC."

"Okay, you a stripper. I never even thought about eating your pu--."

Before he could get the word out of his mouth, she smacked him as hard as she could. His reaction was instantaneous as he grabbed her by the throat and snatched her out of the chair. His fist came up to hit her, but he stopped himself, knowing he could not hit a woman that was carrying his child. He let her neck go as soon as he realized what he had done and that gave Juicy the opening to go crazy.

"Muthafucka'!" she yelled, attacking him with the fork she had been eating with. "Don't you ever touch me again!" she screamed, trying to stab him while he restrained her hands to the sides.

While he pinned her lethal arms down he cooed, "Okay, baby, okay! Settle down, it's cool!"

"It ain't okay! What the fuck does me being a stripper got to do with anything?"

"Nothing Juicy, I'm sorry."

"Nah, tell me what you meant or you'll have to sleep with one eye open nigga!"

"Calm down and I will tell you," he said, laughing at her mean streak. "Girl, you is crazy as hell."

"You ain't seen crazy yet, let me go!" she, demanded yanking away from him.

"Listen, I don't know what kind of niggas you be fucking with, but a nigga not just supposed to eat any and every pussy in front of him. Eating a stripper's pussy is almost equivalent to eating a prostitute pussy, and that's how I been looking at it. Sorry if that offends you," JC explained, backing away from her in case she went all cat woman on him again.

"Fuck you JC. I'm glad to hear I'm just a stripper in your eyes and not your baby momma or your girl for that matter. Nigga, I sleep with you every damn night. Ain't noboby getting any of this pussy, but you, and you don't even appreciate me for that. You must think I'm some kind of hoe or somethin'? Yeah, I strip and show my body off, but I'm smart enough to know that I don't have to fuck to get nigga's money. And I don't just be fucking any and every nigga."

"I can't tell! You fucked me the first day I met you and I was your friend's man."

"Oh, you gonna throw that in my face? I fucked you because I liked you! I knew you didn't want to be with Gloria, because if you did, you wouldn't have been all up and under my skirt. Gloria asked me to try you. The only reason I didn't tell you is that you actually protected me JC, and you didn't even know me. I wanted you more than ever after that. Look what happened? I'm pregnant with your baby, Gloria's dead, and me and you are together." She bursted out in tears. "Just like you was feeling me, I was feeling you. The connection was so strong that I couldn't even give you my number JC. I couldn't do it, I liked you too much, and I couldn't do Gloria like that. This is all just messed up, I swear it is," she said, crying her eyes out. She thought about how screwed up things had been.

JC walked over and hugged her, whispering in her ear, "I'm sorry baby. I really am. It's okay."

After they finished what was left of dinner, JC left and went to the gas station where he called Nino from the telephone booth. He hated talking business on the cell phone.

"What's up," Nino asked after a few rings.

CHAPTER 25

"*W*hat's happening my dude, this JC?"

"What you want to do? You made your mind up yet? I got them for you, hot and ready!"

JC laughed at the pizza reference, "I know, I know. Give me a few days, I'll let you know what's up with that. I got a question for you."

"What's that?"

"I know you familiar with the strippers out here and you was talkin' up that one at the club the other night, remember?"

"Which one?"

"The one called Juicy? You know her?"

"Yeah, I know her. You want the 411 on her? She a cold piece ain't she?"

"Hell yeah. What's the ticket on hittin' somethin' like that?"

"She dances for me a lot and I always call her when I have private parties. She'll trick the shit out of you, making you think you can fuck her. She is freaky as hell dog! Talking all nasty to a nigga, I done seen her play with dildos and everything. One thing I ain't never seen her do is give that pussy away. JC, honest to God I tried to buy that bitch a car for some pussy, that's how horny she had a nigga," he said laughing at himself. "I'm serious, that bitch coulda got a car that night. She wouldn't let me, my man Page, or my boy hit that and these niggas known to be ballers. She strictly business, you better off looking for another freak. She ain't gonna give up that pussy."

"Damn, square business?"

"You didn't like that white bitch Kitten I sent you? Now she'll give you some pussy. That's who you want on your line, young blood!"

"I hit that shit the same night!"

"My man, that's what I'm talking about. That's who you need, cause Juicy ain't giving no head or pussy up. I know this older guy she fucks with. He a loaded white guy. He bought her the car she's driving now, a blue Charger or Challenger, some shit. She still ain't gave his ass any sexual contact. Now the bitch will dance for a nigga, show the pussy, but ain't givin' no play to no one. Right now I think she fuckin' wit this college basketball player, light skinned nigga. I think his name Jason or somethin'. He got that hoe on lock too. Man that bitch be in magazines and all that. I'd marry me a bitch like that!"

JC laughed as Nino ran down the news on Juicy, not having a clue that JC was hitting that shit. JC assumed everyone in Atlanta had fucked her, but that wasn't the case. "Well, maybe I'll stick with Kitten then, she was straight."

"Hell yeah that shit straight. You gotta see these other hoes I be fucking with. Just pretty for no damn reason and all of them like, 21, 22, 23, or 24. Young and wild down here JC. You hear me?"

"Yeah, I hear you. I'ma holla at you soon, we'll get together and make somethin' happen on that other shit."

"Alright, don't wait too long I might have to price gouge a nigga," Nino said, hanging up before JC could say anything.

JC felt better about Juicy, there was no reason for Nino to lie. If anything, he would have built that story up better to pretend he fucked her. JC needed to call them boys up in Ohio and see if they were still in business and if the prices were the same before he bought the bricks off Nino. He pulled into the gas station and pumped the tank full, bought Juicy her favorite watermelon-strawberry juice, and bought some minutes for his phone. On the way out he saw a white Cadillac XLR, drop top, pull up. When the car went beneath the lights, JC's body got chills when he saw the face inside. JC hoped he didn't get seen as he tried to hurry into the car.

"JC! Is that you?" Jamie asked with a big smile on her face. "Where you been with your handsome self?"

"I been around. What you doing out here?"

"My daughter lives out here. I'm just visiting her."

"Oh, that's cool. You been straight?"

"Yeah, I can't complain. You?"

"I'm straight. How long you down here for?"

"A month. I just got here last night so I'm checking things out, getting my bearings. I might stay longer if my daughter, Sabrina, don't get tired of me. She's already talking junk and it hasn't even been 24 hours, but that's kids for you."

JC talked to her for about an hour before telling her he had to get home. "Well, I gotta go. It's been nice seeing you again Jamie."

"You got a number I can get? You know I got some money," she bragged, flashing her platinum credit card.

JC let her down easy and replied, "I wish I could, but I finally found me a good woman. I'm trying to give her the time and respect she deserves."

"Wow, I never thought I would hear you say that, must be nice. I'll see you around in case you change your mind."

JC drove back home wondering what the hell was wrong with him. Jamie had some good ass pussy and money. He just turned her down. Juicy really had him tripping. Whistling a little tune he parked the car and walked up to the door and opened it. The first thing he saw was his bags packed. "Juicy?" he shouted down the hall.

She came walking out of the kitchen with an apron with "MOM" printed on the front. The house smelled like cookies were baking. "What?" she asked with her hands on her hips.

"What the fuck is this? You putting me out?"

"What are we doing JC? Until you learn to treat me like a woman and the mother of your child and not like a stripper you have to go."

"Juicy, I told you I was sorry for saying that and it won't happen again," he said, walking towards her. JC wondered if he had been gone a little longer, would his bags would have been outside. "So you send me to the gas station for a juice and when I come back my shits packed?"

"You lucky, I wasn't going to let you back in at all. And since when does a gas station trip take an hour and a half?"

"I was making some calls on the land line, I don't like using a cell for some things. So this is how yall do it in Atlanta, huh?" he asked, hugging her. He turned around and picked up his bags and carried them to the bedroom. He noticed she even packed his money.

"Hold up! You need to tell me what we're doing before you put any of that back! This wasn't a test."

"What you mean?"

"What I mean is, are we together as one? Am I just a stripper you like to fuck? Am I the mother of your baby and you want us to be together? What? Pick one. I'm tired of playing high school games."

JC couldn't believe she was actually making him choose. "Juicy, we are together as one, okay? You the mother of my child also. I'm sorry for the stripper remark. I'ma do better," he promised her and surprising himself that he meant every word of it.

Juicy looked at him and then said, "Pussy! I was just messing with you. I just wanted to see what you would do seeing your bags all packed up," she said laughing at the look of confusion on his face.

"What?" JC asked when his heart slowed down enough to breathe. "That shit ain't funny Juicy!" he said, chasing her through the house. She took off the apron and threw it back at him to slow his pursuit down. "Why the fuck you playing with me?" he asked when he finally caught her and picked her up. He carried her into the living room and dropped her on the couch where he fell on top of her.

Juicy was still laughing at him, but she was so happy she could burst.

"Will you take me out? Please?" she asked when she could get her breath back.

"After what you just did? Hell nah!"

"Please, I just want to get out before I get so big I won't want to go anywhere."

"Where you want to go?"

"I don't care, somewhere that's not here."

"What do you like to do for fun?"

"What I used to love to do and haven't done in a while is skate."

"You mean like roller skating? Let's go!"

"No, I mean ice skating."

"You gotta show me how to ice skate."

"You ain't ever been ice skating?" JC shook his head no, but if it was anything like roller skating he would be the bomb at it. "I'll show you how," she offered, kissing him on the cheek. She tried to get up but he pulled her back, kissing her on the lips. "Mmmm," she moaned kissing him back. She slid her tongue into his mouth while he massaged her titties until she said, "You on punishment. You ain't sticking your dick in me!"

"Oh yeah?" he asked, flipping her over on her back. "I don't need to stick my dick in you," he said kissing her thighs. The white dress she wore was so short it covered up nothing and as usual she wore no panties.

"You sure you want to start something you're not ready for?" she asked, pulling her dress up and over her head, posing naked for him on the couch. Her body was smooth and soft, like a piece of satin warming up with every touch.

JC couldn't keep his hands off of her. Juicy was not waiting for any preliminary foreplay, she grabbed the back of his head, pushed his face into her pussy and ordered him, "Eat!"

JC went to work, sucking and licking her clit every way he knew how while she moaned. He slid his finger in and out as her juices began to flow. Not used to the personal attention to her pussy, she tapped out and came within two minutes. Her body shook like she had been hit with a stun gun.

When she was done, JC got up off of her and helped her stand up. When Juicy got up, she pushed him down on the couch and said, "My turn now!" And pulled his pants off and sat in between his legs with his fat dick facing her. She wrapped her little mouth around it and began sucking and stroking slowly. Since she could only take so much because of how fat it was, she licked the shaft up and down while sliding her hands across using her saliva as lubrication. She worked his dick like she was twisting a top while popping her mouth on and off the head of his dick. She felt his body tense up which she figured was an indicator that he was ready to cum. She didn't stop, in fact she sped up the motions until JC grabbed her left shoulder and whispered, "Aww, shit!" his fluids spurted out into her mouth. She caught most of it, but there was so much built up it leaked out of her mouth and splattered on his thigh. Juicy swallowed what she could and ended up licking off the rest with her hot little tongue. JC was still turned on, his dick was hard as ever, wanting more, needing more satisfaction. He wanted to be inside her.

Juicy climbed on the couch, and straddled him and guided his dick inside her fiery hole, making her gasp when the full size entered inside her. She took her time letting her body accept him, the girth and length that was waiting to unleash itself onto him. He let her do the work, holding the sides of her hips, watching her tits move like pendulums on a clock movement.

She clenched her pussy muscles as her cunt swallowed his whole dick and then released it as she rode up the shaft like a piston on a car engine.

JC took her pace for as long as he could then his nails dug into her buttocks and he commanded her, "Shit, Juicy!"

CHAPTER 26

*J*uicy picked up the pace and exclaimed in between deep breathe, "I love dis dick!" She bounced on top of his dick until she began to run out of steam, then they reversed positions.JC bent her legs back as far as they could go and put them over his shoulders so her pussy was wide open, then he slid inside her wetness and started stroking her slowly to get into a good groove.

"Fuck me baby!" she begged, as he fucked her harder and faster pounding his dick into her until her moans went from whimpers to groans, pleading for him not to stop. He fucked her for as long as he could, but the nut had built up inside him for too long and soon he exploded inside her seconds before her own orgasm flowed over his dick. He collapsed on top of her with his dick still inside.

"Damn, baby. I'm tired as hell," he said in more of a whisper as he struggled to get his breath back.

Juicy kissed and hugged him close to her, loving how he felt inside her, tickling her pussy. "I love you, JC. You bet not ever leave me," she told him which sounded more like a threat than a request.

"I ain'tgoing no where, girl. You best believe that."

With JC's dick still impaling her, he lifted Juicy up and carried her into the bedroom and fucked her again, going reverse cowgirl and then doggie style. Juicy could barely take him from behind and her noises got the loudest when he tried too.

The next morning, Juicy woke up JC with small kisses all over his face. "You sleep good boo?" she asked, lying on top of him.

"I did, thanks to you," he claimed, running his hands through her hair. "You pretty, even in the morning," JC complimented her, really feeling the love he had for her this morning.

"Thank you. Now see, this is the JC I love. Not the one who be talking shit. Ain't nothing wrong with loving your woman in private. I ain't saying you gotta act all pussy whipped in public, but when it's just you and me, or us and the baby, I want to be feeling you, feeling me."

They talked for more than a half-hour about their future together then JC changed the subject. "Let me ask you something, what happened with you and Jason?"

"He cheated on me, got another girl pregnant. I forgave him for a while, but one day I was just like, I'm good on that."

"How long was you two together?"

"We was together for two years, mostly off and on. He was running with them college bitches when he had away games. I tried to lie to myself, but I knew it inside."

JC kept digging because he wanted to find out where he lived. He was ready to get even with him and his friends. "What did he think about you stripping?"

"He hated it! First he tried to deal with it, then he tried to get me to stop, but I never would. He wasn't trying to be with me though, I was just something to brag about in the locker room, his little stripper arm candy."

"That nigga fucked up! I got you now, and I ain't letting you go," he promised, kissing her. He would continue the conversation later, he didn't want her to get wind of what he was planning. She had enough to worry about.

"You make me feel good JC. I swear I love you so much, you have no idea."

"I love you too baby, for real." They kissed again and again until their lips were locked in a passionate struggle neither one of them willing to relinquish the moment. Juicy took it further and laid completely on top of him and slid his dick into her pussy. They had a non-stop chemistry for each other, insatiable in every way. JC couldn't keep his dick out of her and if it were possible to get her pregnant while she was already pregnant they would have had quadruplets over the past 24 hours. He fucked her in the bedroom, which spilled into the shower, then snacking on each other in the kitchen, fucking in the living room again, to the dining room table, and even inside of the walk-in closet.

They were very random with their sex life, they had gone to the movies where she sucked his dick dry, he banged her in the bowling alley bathroom, he took her skating and fucked Juicy in the dressing room with her skates still on, he fingered her in the restaurant until she nearly passed out trying not to moan. They were doing whatever came to mind no matter where they were.

She always danced for him like she did at the club, bringing herself to an orgasm right in front of his face without him even needing to touch her. It was a show he could watch over and over.

The weeks passed by quickly and she was beginning to show more and more in her stomach. He realized he was running out of money and he had to get out of the house and make some kind of cash flow happen. JC drove to the tint shop in Juicy's Challenger and had the tint added while the rims were taken off. It was like a whole different car. Juicy was so well known as a top of the line stripper, and even in a big city like Atlanta, her car was known too, at least with the tinting no one could see who was inside the car. JC noticed that since Juicy had been with him she had faded out of the spotlight because she was busy with him. When magazines called for her to pose, their pleas went straight to voicemail. When Nino called to book her for parties, she ignored their offers. She checked out from everyone except her mother. Maybe it was the pregnancy that brought them closer together. Along with her closeness with her mom, came her little sister and brother. Juicy felt very matronly and protective now that she was pregnant.

While Juicy was taking care of the tinting, JC waited in the office talking to the sensuous receptionist. She was a dark caramel color, nice petite body, with short hair, and a strong country accent. As he was talking to the sexy young thing, a woman walked up from behind holding a bag of food from a restaurant with a big smile on her face. "JC, what are you doing talking to my daughter?" Jamie asked, handing the food past him to her daughter.

JC turned around to see Jamie. "This your daughter, Jamie? No wonder she's so beautiful," he complimented both of them.

"Mom? You know him?" her daughter asked with a disgusted look on her face. She was well aware of her mother's reputation as a local cougar who loved young guys, which is where she figured this young black man knew her mom from.

"Yes, JC is a friend of mine. He's handsome, right?" Jamie asked, standing close to JC, almost sitting on him. Jamie's daughter forced a smile and left them standing there while she went to go eat. It was gross enough to watch her mom flirt, she couldn't stand it while she ate.

JC couldn't help but notice the way the blue jeans Jamie wore hugged her body. She was still as fit as hell. She might even have lost a little weight. JC wondered if she was working out or just fucking a lot.

Jamie sat down in her daughter's vacated seat and said, "So we meet again. You ready to give me your number? I have cash on me today," she said, reaching into her Louis Vuitton bag and pulled out a couple of G's in $50 dollar bills. "Put this in your pocket for now, in case you change your mind," she stated pushing the money deep into his pockets, making sure her fingers touched his dick on the way down. "Hmmm, I do miss you," she added purring like a lioness.

"Jamie, I told you I--."

CHAPTER 27

*J*amie cut him off before he could reject her again, "JC, don't do this to me. Don't act like you don't want me. I have some rich friends down here who are willing to spend good money. If you're willing, it could be some extra money for you."

"I don't need money like that, Jamie. I need car seats, cribs, and shit like that. I can't be fucking for a thousand or two anymore, I gotta think long term. I got a baby on the way, I need to be investing. This little shit ain't worth the time or effort I'ma have to put in, not to mention the risk if my girl find out. You feel me?"

"Well, what is worth your time these days? Oh, and energy," she asked, smiling as she remembered that big black, fat dick inside her pussy. The thought of it made her tingle inside.

"I want $5,000 for this dick Jamie. I'm sorry. If your girls ain't down wit that, find another young dude."

"Oh, no. That's fine, they'll pay that, I know they will. For me, I get a little discount since I'm setting this up for you. Like you said, it's an investment. I already told them about you and they can't wait to try you out. You gonna be the talk of Atlanta. Trust me, give me the number JC or I'll give you mine and I'ma make you, your girl, and your baby a lot of money."

Despite his earlier reservations, he liked the sound of that, five G's each time he had to sling his dick. They exchanged numbers and she asked him to meet her later at a hotel room. He was going to have to think of some story to tell Juicy about where he was going.

"What's on your mind JC?" Juicy asked, when they were in the car on the way home.

"What you mean?"

"I mean, what's got you so quiet? You been this way since before we left the tint shop."

"Thinking of money and ways to make it, so we set. I was wondering if I should sell a little dope to build up a nice chunk of bread for us. You know anyone that be buying cane at big quantities down here? I know some people in Ohio, but I ain't feeling that Fed beef about going over state lines and shit."

Juicy was initially shocked, but one name did come to mind. "I really don't want you to be messing with that stuff JC, but I do know this one guy you would be safe with. But there's others out there around the clubs, I'm not introducing you to them, they be robbing muthafucka's. I been knowing this one guy since high school. He was my gym teacher then. I'll call him later for you if you want."

"Cool, thanks. I know you don't want me messin' wit this stuff, but I gotta make sure you and the baby straight at all times." This was a good start. He was glad she didn't give no hassle or long lecture. He didn't want her to be sweating him every time he went out and she must have known that. When they got home, he went to his stash and counted out what he had left. A

WOMEN LIE MEN LIE - PART 3

little over $64,000, thanks to the two grand Jamie had given him.

Juicy walked in and saw he had emptied the whole box of money. "You taking it all? How much you buying?"

"A few keys right now."

"Right now?"

"Yeah, why?"

"Well, let me call Brad first and let him know what's going on so you won't have to sit on it."

"Good idea. Look at you all God fathering up for a nigga!" he said, laughing as he packed the money into the gym bag.

"Hey, I gotta make sure you good. Besides, we got rent due in like four days."

"We good baby. Go make that call." While Juicy was on her phone with Brad, JC called up Nino and told him he'd meet him at 7 p.m. He asked for two keys and planned to meet at the hotel Jamie was staying at.

"Brad said he'll pay $29,000 a piece, that's good for you?"

"Yeah, that's straight for now."

Later that evening, around 6:30, JC headed out to meet Nino. "I'll call you before I get there and after the deal goes down in case anything goes wrong," JC told Juicy, giving her a kiss.

Nino armed all five of the guys he was sending to meet JC with AK's and pistol. "How you want it, Nino?" his cousin, T-Money asked.

"Tear his ass to pieces, don't even play. I want the whole car shredded like cheese, then I want you to set it on fire," Nino answered him, loading the clips with fresh bullets. He hated letting someone else get the clips ready. More times than not they jammed on him and JC was not the one he wanted to be in front of when his gun jammed.

"Damn, what you got against this mutha fucka? He must have done some grimy shit to you, huh?"

"He did, he's the reason I moved to Atlanta. He killed half my damn crew. He think he slick and he thinks I don't know it was him. Then he robbed them taking my fucking money. He ain't call me or give me anything," Nino recounted the story for his crew, getting pissed all over again.

"I got you, cuz. Don't even trip, I know what to do."

"I want to hear this shit on the news and tape it so I can remember how I got that bitch!"

"So what's the play," T-Money asked.

"He wants to meet at a hotel, but I'ma call him and change it, tell him there's cops around. Then have him park on the side of a street and have him wait on me. All you gotta do is drive by and spray the car up. I don't want no drive-by either, that's how you miss a nigga. I want you to stop and spray the car until the clips are empty, then burn his ass up," Nino said, smiling as he thought of how the scene would play out and look.

"You going?" he asked, putting on his jacket and making sure the ski mask was in the pocket.

"Hell yes, I'm coming. I gotta see this shit," Nino said. "The street I'ma have him meet me on is in an area the police don't even come down. So you don't have to worry, you'll have time, but make sure you get the money!"

Nino drove the car and called JC on his cell, "What up, my dude? Where you at?"

"I'm almost at the hotel. Why? What up?"

"Look, my boys did a drive-by and said there's a couple of cop cars at the hotel, looks like an accident or something. Let's flip the meet somewhere a little more quiet, okay?"

"Yeah, that's straight. We don't need no interruptions, not tonight. What you driving?"

"I'm in a black Towncar. Meet me on the corner of Parks and Dantley Drive. There's an abandoned warehouse where no one goes, I'll find you. Keep the lights off." Nino said.

"Alright, hurry up though, I got shit to do. See you in fifteen."

"Hey, what you driving?" Nino asked, keeping him on the line so he could get there first and set up the hit.

"I'm driving a blue Challenger with tinted windows," JC answered, putting in the street names for the GPS.

CHAPTER 28

"*B*e careful, they got punks running around this area trying to rob a nigga."

"I'll be careful, best believe that," JC said, patting the gym bag next to him.

"I'll see you in a minute," Nino said, hanging up. "I got that nigga."

Nino and his team were about ten minutes away and couldn't take a chance on speeding with the guns in the car. Nino's phone rang, it was JC again. "He's probably wondering where we at. We're coming, dog, don't worry about that," Nino said to his crew who all started laughing.

As Nino was turning onto the street JC called again, "Hey, where you at? I can't just be sitting in this area all day."

"I'm right here," Nino responded hanging up the phone as his guys jumped out and let off a barrage of bullets shredding the Challenger from front to back and top to bottom. Shots rang out for two full minutes until the clips went empty amid a cloud of smoke and littered shells beneath their feet.

T-Money grabbed a pre-made moltov cocktail and lit it, throwing the burning projectile through the back window to smoke JC out if he survived the bullets. The car had so many holes in it there was no way a human could have survived. Nino wanted to make sure there was no chance of JC living or getting away. Nino felt a little quilt afterwards, but he couldn't let JC live after betraying him the way he did in Michigan.

Kelly flew back to Michigan after being unable to hunt down JC. The city of Atlanta was too big and who knows if he was even still there. To make herself feel better she traded in her truck and pulled out of the dealership in a brand new Jaguar. She closed down a few of her houses due to JC being on the loose and not knowing if he was hunting them while they were hunting him. Kelly didn't want her girls going through the drama, so she bought a five bedroom house in West Bloomfield, a four bedroom house in Bay City, and a six bedroom house in Dearborn. Business had been good for Kelly, and although the economy was horrible for most everyone else, pussy was selling. That was the difference in the dope game. You could only sell dope once and it was gone, pussy you could sell over and over.

Since the death of her baby daddy, Marvin, Kelly had hardly dated anyone. She instead turned her sexual frustrations into growing the business and now she was ready to expand to other states.

When Kelly arrived at the West Bloomfield house, all the girls were out at appointments except for one, Lily, who was busy at the computer when Kelly walked in. Lily was an Asian girl whose age was difficult to discern, but she was tall with almond colored eyes, long jet black hair, and small breasts for the men and women who had Asian fetishes.

"Hi, Kelly. You scared me," Lily told her, turning around.

"Sorry, what's going on?"

"I'm headed out to an appointment in a sec, but I'm glad I saw you. Cody left you something in case he wasn't here when you arrived," she said, leaving the room and returning a few seconds later with an envelope.

"Thanks," Kelly answered, putting the envelope in her purse. Cody had been Kelly's go to driver since her brother had been murdered.

After talking to Lily for a few more minutes, Kelly made stops in Dearborn and Bay City. In all, she picked up 16 thousand dollars to go with the 21 thousand yesterday. It's why she was so willing to close down the houses in questionable neighborhoods, she couldn't allow the police or gang violence to halt her money flow, she had too many people depending on her.

———

Jamie went to go pick up JC after he called her. He was sweating something fierce when he got inside her car. When she asked him what had happened he could barely tell her. The bottle of water had saved his life. When he called Nino earlier to ask where he was, he had walked to the party store two blocks from the abandoned warehouse. He was about to tell Nino that when he hung up in his face, then the bullets flew into the empty Challenger. JC borrowed a couple more thousand from Jamie and told her he'd see her later tonight as she dropped him off at Juicy's house. JC was a little afraid to walk in and face Juicy. He called to have her report the car stolen, he didn't tell her why.

"What the hell happened, JC?" Juicy demanded.

He had to sit down and get his thoughts together. His mind was racing, trying to catch up with all that had just happened. He was so pissed, ready to kill anything or anyone who got in his way. "That nigga tried to kill me," is how JC responded to her question.

"Who tried to kill you? The people that was after you?"

"Nah, the person I went to go meet and buy the coke from," he said, trying to stay calm with her, then a light bulb went off. "We gotta get out of here ASAP! If they see your name on the news, they'll know I didn't die and try to finish the job by coming here. Nino will be after us baby. We gotta go right now," he said, standing up. Pack as fast as you can, taking only what you really need. A few changes of clothes, credit cards, cash, jewelry."

"Where are we gonna go JC!" Juicy asked confused and scared.

"We'll get a room for now. Call the rental place and have a car delivered here right now. Go Juicy! I ain't got time to explain anymore!"

Juicy jumped into gear, trusting that JC knew best. She called the rental place and ordered a truck on her credit card and then she started to pack. Once he told her the car was shot up, she began to second guess having JC stay. She was fleeing her own home when she had done nothing wrong, just fell for the wrong kind of guy.

Two hours later, they were inside a hotel room where they paid cash and parked the truck in a hotel across the street in case Nino had people who could get credit card activity checked. Juicy was sick about the fact that she had to leave so many of her things behind. Things she had worked so hard to get. "What happened to the money JC?"

JC could only shake his head, "It's gone. I left it in the car. I didn't want to carry it in the store and I was only gonna be gone for a minute. I didn't see this coming Juicy."

Juicy fell to her knees, overcome with fear. "Oh my God, JC," she cried out, as tears poured from worried eyes.

Although JC was mad at the world and himself, he knelt down next to her, wanting to comfort his girl. JC held Juicy in his arms until her tears subsided. "Don't worry baby. I'ma make up for it, I promise. I'ma get it all back," JC vowed, wanting to cry right beside her, but he fought to stay strong.

They watched the news and Juicy gasped with shock when she saw what was left of her car. By the time the fire department had made it to the scene, the fire had burned itself out. Only a metal shell remained. A shell packed with hundreds of bullet holes. It turned JC's stomach to realize how close he came to being inside. He knew he had to go hard and respond. He was done playing games and hiding. The news ended the story by confirming no one was found inside the vehicle and police were investigating who had stolen the car and where they were now. JC apologized to Juicy about the car, but she had insurance on it, so she would be able to get another one in a month or so. By the time midnight came, Juicy had cried herself to sleep and JC called Jamie to come pick him up. He didn't want to be in the truck right now in case someone was already watching it. He made a mental note to have the rental place come pick it up in the morning. When they got to Jamie's room, there was another older white lady waiting for them, she was probably in her late forties and after Jamie introduced them, they exchanged numbers and she promised to be in touch with JC real soon.

When she left, it was just JC and Jamie like old times. "Have you missed me JC?" Jamie asked, as she began to unbutton her shirt. Jamie was looking good and JC could tell she had been hitting the gym trying to stop the inevitable sagging from stopping her cougar status. She had both their clothes off in minutes and JC began to punish her from behind as she yelled out in pain and passion. He had no sympathy as he took out his revenge on her aging pussy. It took him an hour to get his nut off while she had two during the same span. JC wanted to kill everyone who had fucked him over and he slapped at her ass with each thrust until her cheeks were bright red. JC was done waiting for the right time to do things, he was about to go after them all, fearless. He didn't even feel alive the way he was living, ducking and dodging mutha fucka's. After he got done fucking the shit out of Jamie, he went into the bathroom and flushed his condom then jumped into the shower to clean off. He had no time to cuddle with her, that's what Juicy was for. He got his money and left in the middle of Jamie begging him to stay the night. When she realized he wasn't going to stay, she tried to make things right and kissed him goodbye and asked for more of his time tomorrow. JC had never fucked her like he did tonight and he doubted she would be ready after she woke up in the morning, walking like she had been horseback riding all week.

The first target on JC's list was Juicy's ex-boyfriend, Jason. He got the address from an old bill, still in Juicy's dresser drawer. He navigated himself there without a plan of how he was going to go about this. He had also stolen his phone number from Juicy's phone while she slept. When he arrived at Jason's place, he saw the truck he'd driven the day he attacked JC sitting in the driveway. JC looked in the truck and saw a blinking blue light inside, indicating the alarm was on. He set the alarm off by trying to open the door and then hugged the side of the house for when Jason came out. He heard the blinds move to the side as Jason looked out to see who or what had set the alarm off, then he came outside with no shirt on. JC had his gun pointed right at his head. It looked like he wanted to run, but with the gun so close he was too scared to move.

"Yeah, nigga! You bet not move. I'll put a slug deep inside that dumb ass head. Where's the other bitches you had wit you?" JC asked, tapping him in the back of the head with the heavy steel barrel.

"They ain't here, just me and and a girl," he stuttered.

JC patted him down for a weapon and found small knots of money. "Probably thought you wouldn't see me again, huh? Open the door and go inside, slowly," JC ordered him, making sure the gun stayed against his back. "Where she at? Tell her to come here, pussy."

"Kitten, come here!"

"Kitten the stripper?" JC asked shocked to find her here with Juicy's ex.

"Yes, sir!" Jason replied with his voice trembling in fear.

"Yes, sir? You got some guns in the house? And don't even think of lying to me."

"Nah, I don't do guns. I'm a star basketball player. I don't want any problems, sir!"

"You don't want no problems, but you and your bitch ass friends wanna jump a nigga? You was tough as hell when you was wit them, remember that?" JC asked, as Kitten came out of the back room with a two piece, red lingerie set on.

"Kitten, sit on the couch and don't move," JC commanded her.

CHAPTER 29

She saw JC's gun and did exactly as he said. "JC, right?" she asked, feeling cold all of a sudden.

"Yeah, hoe. We know each other. Aren't you Juicy's good friend? What the hell you doing fucking her ex? Don't you girls got a code against that or something?"

"I—I."

"I nothing! Shut up and stay seated. You go sit next to her too, nigga," JC said, pushing Jason on the couch beside her. "You two make any crazy moves and you both dead, simple as that," JC warned pointing gun back and forth at them. Jason had his hands in the air like he was being arrested. "Put your hands down, stupid." JC could tell this was a new experience for Jason. He had probably never been robbed before. "You got some money in this crib?"

"I got about $2,500 in my room in the shoe box on the closet shelf. Look man, I'm sorry about what happen."

"Did I ask for an apology?" JC knew he was going to have to kill them both. "Kitten, I'll holla at you," he said, making her

167

think he was letting her go, but two bullets from JC's gun pushed her back onto the navy blue couch. Her body jerked for a second and then she tilted her head into Jason's lap, like she was giving him some head from the grave.

"Oh, shit! Come on, man! Please! I can get you more money!" Jason begged, trying to get away from the bleeding Kitten. Tears welled up in his eyes when he saw his first dead body.

"Shut the fuck up before you be next!"

Jason nodded his head, wanting to believe he would be able to live. "Get your punk ass up and show me where that money at and take off that chain you wearing, too." Jason went into the bedroom, gave JC the cash and chain and waited. He even offered his one carat earrings, but JC knocked them onto the floor. "I don't want that shit, bitch. Now get on the bed and lay down!"

Jason laid down and began pleading again, "I'm sorry, sir. I really am. I go to church every Sunday and think about what I did to you. I just love Juicy so much."

"You know you fucked up don't you? Now get some paper and write down the addresses to those other bitches that rode wit you." JC watched him write the addresses down and said, "You a real bitch. Where's all the tough guy shit from the other day?"

"I'm not like that, really. I do that for attention from my boys or for girls," he whined, handing JC the paper.

"Oh, so you like to showoff, huh?"

"I don't want to, but I just want them to like me."

"Stand up and turn around. I'ma give you something to really brag about, I'ma shoot you in the ass. Up against the wall and spread 'em."

JC waited until Jason did as ordered and put the barrel to his left ass cheek and pulled the trigger. "Ahhh shiit!!!"

Jason shouted, falling to the floor holding his ass. "Please, I learned my lesson!"

Even though he was enjoying himself, JC was growing tired of playing with Jason and raised the barrel at point blank range and blew his face off. The shot made quite the artistic impression as blood and brain matter splattered against the white paint behind where he was standing. JC walked out the door, leaving them both to be found by the neighbors.

JC made it back before the sun was up and he undressed and laid next to Juicy who was still sleeping. As soon as he felt Juicy move he woke up, a few hours later.

"Relax, baby," she whispered, "You was jumping in your sleep."

"I was?"

"Yeah, you scared me. I thought you was having a seizure or something."

"What time is it," he asked, trying to wipe the sleep from his eyes.

"Quarter to eight."

"Go back to sleep baby. I won't jump no more," he promised only half awake. "I love you."

"I love you too."

Juicy couldn't resist and climbed on top and started humping him while still kissing his lips. JC was only wearing boxer shorts and his dick was sticking out the side of them, so he tore them off while she rode at a slow pace, like she was horseback riding across the fields. It lasted nearly an hour before she

A. ROY MILLIGAN

finally had an orgasm, then she continued rocking on his dick until he came as well. Juicy laid on his chest listening to his heartbeat as he fell into a peaceful sleep. She needed answers to her questions.

As the sun came through the side of the drapes, Juicy woke up and saw it was past noon. JC was still lying naked next to her. She snuggled up next to him and ran her finger over the bullet holes that scarred his chest.

When JC mumbled in his sleep she asked, "So what are we gonna do baby?"

"We gonna get our shit together and you gonna have my baby in peace. I don't want you worrying about anything, Juicy. I know it looks bad right now, but I need you to trust me. And believe me when I say everything is going to be okay."

"I do, but-."

"There shouldn't be any buts. All I want you to do is have this baby, okay? Let me deal with the rest the way I know how."

Juicy listened and wanted to believe in him, but to her things were falling apart and fast. People were trying to kill her baby daddy. She had to move from her place and her bank account was also getting low. "I'll try not to stress JC. I trust you."

"Please do. I got us. You just let me work and put this shit back together."

"What you mean by that? What are you gonna do?"

"See, there you go, worrying about shit other than the baby. I want you to go to your mom's house instead of staying in this hotel all day every day."

"I want to stay with you JC."

"I need you to go to your mom's right now. I'll work better and faster if I don't have to worry about you. I'ma come see you each day and do whatever you need me to do. I just can't be leaving you in a hotel room all pregnant and shit."

"I'm fine JC--."

"Juicy...will you please go to your moms for me, just for a little while. We'll find a new place, a place we can move to in about a month. Use your mom's credit, not yours."

"Are you sure JC? I don't like this one bit."

"Yes, I'm sure," he answered, handing over most his cash to her. "While I'm out in the streets doing my thing, you gonna be holding the money, okay? And don't be spending it unless it's for the baby."

"Ok, how much is this and where did you get it?"

"Too many questions baby. Just take it and hold on to it."

An hour later, Juicy was sent to her mom's in a taxi after calling the rental place to pick up the truck. JC took another taxi to Jamie's hotel, calling ahead so she was waiting for him and his dick. When JC arrived, she opened the door naked as the day she was born. She started kissing JC like she hadn't seen him for months. Without any preliminaries, JC got busy fucking her, after all it was a business deal, not love. He banged her three different ways, ate her pussy while fingering her asshole. Jamie went through four orgasms in a span of an hour. When he was done, he went to take a shower and Jamie followed him wanting more and he gave it to her so hard, she had tears in her eyes when she came. "Oh Lord, boy! What's gotten into you?"

"You like that shit, huh?"

"Like is not the word. What you gave me in Michigan was one thing, but this on a whole different level. You gonna make me stay in Atlanta longer than I planned."

"That will be perfect. I want you to stay."

"You do?" she asked, coming over and hugging him.

JC told her what she wanted to hear, it was what all women wanted to hear that they were wanted and needed. She had plenty of money, so why not string her along. Although she was married, she loved his dick, dick she couldn't get in her matrimonial bed. Being successful was one thing, but good dick was hard to find in her world and like anything else in life, if you wanted the best, you had to pay for it.

"When you coming back?"

"I'll be back later, I got some things to do, including looking for a condo for me and my baby mama."

"Can I come with you? I know real estate people and what's being over-priced."

"Sure, come on if you want. But you're never to come to the condo after we buy it, don't get shit twisted Jamie."

CHAPTER 30

$\mathcal{W}$ hile Jamie and JC were out looking for condos, Jamie's friend called and wanted to see JC tonight. JC made an appointment at midnight. Jamie was happy for him, although she wanted him one more time today. Juicy called him several times throughout the day and each time he had Jamie pull over while he got out of the car to talk to her. JC told Juicy he was out looking at condos which made her excited, but they would need a co-signer since neither of them had jobs or cash up front. Juicy knew a sugar daddy who would put his name on anything for her without sex, she told JC in case he was thinking anything else.

Jamie found them a cozy two bedroom condo that he liked. They were asking $75,000, and he was hoping to get Jamie to at least furnish the place. Jamie didn't care about helping him, she knew her place and she assured him that she wouldn't do anything to mess things up for him. They went back to her hotel after Jamie fronted the down payment to hold the property until Juicy got her sugar daddy to come co-sign the paperwork. He fucked Jamie one more time, but then was forced to drink two energy drinks after Juicy called and said her mom was gone for a few hours. He fucked Juicy, ate her and she fell into a contented sleep. JC went and checked into a different hotel, took a shower and laid down to take a quick power nap before he had to be at Jamie's friend, Linda's house.

On the way there, JC called Nino to see if he would answer, he did.

"What happened man?"

"You missed, that's what happened."

"What you mean? I d-."

"Come on man. Don't play me like I'm stupid. You tried to kill me and since you missed, it's your ass nigga!"

"Fuck you!" Nino said hanging up on JC.

JC laughed into the dead phone, he was going to enjoy killing Nino.

Linda lived further out than JC expected. He had never been to this part of Atlanta before. He pulled up to her gated mansion and pressed the buzzer, it was 12 a.m. when the gate swung open and he drove up a circular drive with an impressive water fountain out front with statues of two, well hung young men peeing into the fountain. The mansion was a brick cream color with turrets on the side like at a castle. The front door was solid oak with an ornate knocker in the middle of the door. JC was about to use it when he noticed a camera in the corner swing over to face him and then the door unlocked from inside, allowing him access. Unbeknownst to him, Linda had been watching him on the security monitors since he pulled up. She saw the excitement in his eyes when he looked at the antique cars parked in the drive, and the size of her house. She loved seeing how people would respond to the luxury of her place.

"Hi JC. It's okay you can relax. There's no one here but my daughter."

"Nice place Linda! Damn." Linda was wearing a gold silk gown and was bare foot on the tiled floor. He assumed the floors were heated. She was around 5'4" and had a gymnast's body. Her husband was killed years ago in a plane accident and rather than tie herself down in a serious relationship with someone chasing after her money, she just used escort services and paid different men to sleep with her. It was much more convenient for her busy schedule. Her husband had bought several types of businesses over the years and when he died, she learned each one of them so she wasn't dependent on any man.

JC liked her look, nothing gave away her age. Her hair was dark brown with big curls that caressed the back of her shoulder blade. It didn't take much conversation to get JC into her bed where she began sucking his dick before he had a chance to get his clothes all the way off. While her mouth engulfed much of his dick, JC looked around this freaks bedroom, with a sex swing in the corner, bars above the bed, and sex toys on the dresser. Before JC could cum from her giving him head, she pulled a condom onto his dick that felt unusual from the normal ones he used. This condom felt wet on the inside and super thin as it warmed up upon contact with his dick. When she impaled herself onto his cock, the thing got hotter. Linda held onto the bars for support as she rode him, moaning softly with her huge tits bouncing up and down. Her body moved like a snake as she fucked him, leading them both to satisfying orgasms.

In the midst of changing positions, she asked him to stay the night which JC had no problem with as long as she understood it was going to be extra. She simply smiled in response and threw her hair back as she began sucking his dick again before taking it in the ass.

Linda had more energy than he expected, but he was having fun with her flexibility. He never realized he could fuck a girl in so many ways, she was like a living Karma Sutra. She even let JC fuck her while a dildo vibrated in her ass, once again pleasuring them both because JC could feel the vibration all the way up his dick.

By 4 a.m., Linda had fallen asleep and JC was wide awake. He had a hard time sleeping next to someone he didn't know, so he got up and began looking for the kitchen to get something to eat. The mansion had so many doors he didn't know where to go, so he began opening random doors. As he stopped in front of another entry way downstairs, he heard moans coming from behind the door. He cracked the door slightly until he saw a woman lying in bed completely naked, legs wide open, watching a porno while she shoved a medium sized black dildo in and out of her pussy. JC knew he should leave, but he couldn't move as she continued to moan and pleasure herself. He was concentrating on her bad pussy when she startled him and asked, "Who are you?" not in the least embarrassed at being caught.

"Ahh... JC, a friend of Linda's. Who are you?"

She smiled a knowing smile and said, "My mom's friend? She has a lot of friends like you," she added scooting off the bed.

"I didn't mean to startle you, I was looking for the kitchen."

"You sure? My room doesn't look like a kitchen unless you're talking about my oven."

JC chuckled and said, "Nah, my bad," as he moved out the door.

"Where you going now, to look for the bathroom?"

"To find the kitchen."

"I'll show you where it is," she replied, brushing up against him as she walked past. She looked like a younger version of her mom, but her tits and ass were tighter. She grabbed his hand and led him into the kitchen. "How long you known my mom?"

"Umm, I just met her," JC answered, looking at her titties. It was clear she had implants, they were too perfect.

"You like what you see?" she asked, opening fridge so the light gave him a better view.

"Yeah, why wouldn't I? You have a nice body. Them real?"

She giggled, covering her mouth so she didn't wake her mom, "No, but they feel real. Touch 'em," she offered, taking his hand and putting it on her right breast. "Squeeze it softly," she ordered him.

"Damn, they do feel real."

She turned around and jammed her ass against his dick that was covered by boxers, "Go ahead stick your dick in me."

JC swallowed nervously, not sure he heard her right, "What?" he asked, as his dick betrayed him and jumped to attention.

"Stick your dick in me," she repeated, spreading her ass cheeks open with her hands while her head was almost resting against some left over dish.

"I don't have a condom. You got one?"

In response she yanked his boxers down and guided his dick into the entrance of her pussy, "Fuck me, now! Stick it in me."

His dick got even harder as he plunged into her and started moving it back and forth while she held on to the inside on the fridge door handle. Her pussy was extra slippery and soft, causing JC to cum fast, all over her back. She turned around and sucked the rest of the cum from his dick. "Well, this is the kitchen, get what you want. You know where my room is the next time you visit. Let me know if you need to be shown where the bathroom is," and she walked away.

Shaking his head in confusion about what just took place, JC didn't even bother getting a glass and drank orange juice from the bottle while eating some turkey slices without bread. On his way back to Linda's room, he stopped by who he assumed was her daughter's room which was not that far from the kitchen. He wondered how many other men she had fucked when they too were looking for the kitchen.

"What are we looking for now, the garage?" she asked, looking up from the computer she was on, still naked.

"No, what's your name?"

"Oh, Sandra."

"You are eighteen, right?"

"Nice time to ask, maybe I am," she teased, looking at the worried expression on his face. "I'm 21, don't worry! You're not going to jail for fucking me. And your name is?"

"JC, nice to meet you. Sandra."

She went back to typing, clearly dismissing him, so he walked upstairs to Linda's room and crept back into bed and dozed off. He woke up sometime the next morning with Linda sucking his dick between licking his balls. "Oh, shit!" was all he could get out as she stroked his dick with her hand that was coated with some type of gel that almost had JC climbing the wall. The suction was so strong that when he came, it shot straight out of his dick and three inches into the air. Linda tried to catch it on the way down in her mouth, but it splattered mostly on her face. JC's toes curled as she sucked the rest out of him.

"Damn, Linda," was all he could say, as he lay there trying to think of when the last time he nutted that good.

Before JC left, she handed him an envelope with all hundreds inside. He counted it as soon as he got inside the car, he had Jamie rent for her. He was trying hard to stay off the grid so Lamoto or Nino couldn't just walk up on him and catch him unprepared. Once he counted to $5,000, he noticed she had stuffed in several more hundreds. When he arrived back at the hotel, he received a text message from Linda.

From Linda: JC, you were great! I know Jamie gave her other friends your number, but I want to purchase you exclusively, so you don't have to go anywhere else. I can take care of you past your wildest imagination and all I want from you is that delicious dick that you gave me last night when I want it. I'm a very wealthy woman and I can take care of you and your family, if only you'll take care of me too. Thanks for a great night. See you later tonight, at the same time.

The text kind of sent chills down his body, but he was more than happy, he just wasn't sure if he wanted to be tied to one girl on the side. Women got crazy when they thought you were with them exclusively. He fell asleep, dreaming of all the money Linda would give him. He woke up to Juicy calling him at almost noon.

"Hello?" he answered in an exhausted sounding voice.

"Good morning baby."

"Good morning Juicy, what's up?"

"I miss you, I'm coming to see you."

"Yeah, but didn't I tell you to stay away from me? Let me come to you baby."

"I'll be there in a half-hour!" she announced, hanging up.

CHAPTER 31

*J*C jumped up and dove into the shower to wash his dick off and then fell back to sleep waiting for her. When her knock woke him up, they ate breakfast together and looked at the condo online that he had picked for them. Then she saw the envelope filled with hundreds in his pants pocket lying on the floor.

"Where you get this?" she asked, pulling out all the hundred dollar bills. "Are these all hundreds?"

"Yeah, they all hundreds. What you think they fake?" he asked, as she held them to the light.

"Just checking you ain't running no counterfeit ring. How much is it and you ain't answered my question about where you got it?"

"I don't know, at least five grand, count it if you want."

She did and it tallied up to $8,000. "Take it with you, I'll have more tomorrow," he promised.

"JC, where-."

"I told you to stop asking all them questions. Just trust me, okay?" he asked, eating a piece of bacon.

She shook her head and replied, "I don't know how you expect me not to ask questions when I'm carrying your baby. I worry when I'm not with you. How do I know you ain't doing no stick-ups out there, robbing folks?"

"I ain't jacking nobody, it's check cashing money if you must know."

"What does that mean?"

"Fake checks. I send people into banks to cash fake checks."

"Damn, really?"

Juicy let the matter rest after that, she was satisfied that he wouldn't be gunned down in some daring bank robbery. They drove to a nearby park and took their shoes off and walked barefoot in the grass, talking about their future and possible baby names. JC bought them both an ice cream cone and they sat around watching the other kids playing, they could easily imagine it were their kids they were watching. The scene moved them so much that as soon as they got back to the room, JC got busy eating her pussy and then she sucked his dick, not anything like what Linda did for him last night, but they were both satisfied. She left soon afterwards, feeling better than she had when she arrived. JC had some calls to make and money was to be made and it wasn't getting made in this hotel room. He found an unknown caller on his phone and when he returned the call a female voice answered.

"Hello?"

"Did someone call for JC?"

"Yes, JC. This is Stephanie, a friend of Jamie's, love. She told me to contact you when I was feeling lonely, so tonight I'm feeling extra lonely. Do you think you could help a girl out?" she asked with a strong British accent.

"Oh, yeah? Well I think I can fill a couple of hours of your time," JC answered, forgetting all about Linda's offer. Stephanie gave JC her address to an apartment only twenty minutes away. JC called her when he parked his car and she was waiting at the door for him when he arrived. He almost turned around and ran when he saw her, but instead he kept his composure and said, "Wait a minute. I forgot something in the car, I'll be right back." He called Jamie when he was out of sight.

"Hello dear."

"What the hell is wrong with you?" he asked.

"What are you talking about, calm down?"

"Why didn't you tell me Stephanie's a midget?"

"I didn't think it mattered, besides the size of her bank account? She's going to pay $5,000. That's not a cheap call for her to make and you better go make that money."

JC thought about it for a minute, thinking of Juicy and his baby, "Yeah, alright. But next time you need to tell me what's going on."

"Okay, I'm sorry. Have fun!"

JC took a deep breath and walked back in. "Sorry about that, I forgot to make a phone call. How you doing girl?" he asked, flashing his white teeth. "You looking sexy as hell."

"Thank you. I was worried you wasn't coming back. You look sexy too. You drink?"

JC was looking at her from the corner of his eye while looking around the apartment, she was big and round, but like four foot tall. Everything in her apartment was made to fit her height. The fridge was also about four foot tall, along with the stove and counters in the kitchen. "Yeah, what you got?" "I got it all, and if I don't have it I can get it sent up. Look in those two end cabinets."

JC found a nice looking decanter of cognac and began drinking straight from the bottle. Stephanie was beginning to look sexier with every sip he took. When he followed her to the bedroom he continued to drink. He didn't want to get drunk, but he did want a decent buzz to be able to perform on her little body.

Stephanie climbed on the bed and began giving him a message, "So how do you want it baby?" JC asked her, enjoying her hands on his back.

"You tell me," she answered, letting him undress her. First, to go was the black skirt, then the yellow blouse, and finally her titties popped out of her bra. She had a decent size rack for someone of her small stature. He pulled her black lacy underwear to the side and began sliding his finger into her hairy pussy. Stephanie started to moan louder and louder, and by the time a second finger joined the first one, she was getting super wet and said, "Yeah, fuck this pussy!" while she swiveled her waist back and forth, forcing his fingers further in.

JC was surprised by how outspoken and open she was, "Oh, shit! Oh, shit," she squealed, after his strokes went faster and harder into her pussy, then JC saw when he pulled out he had her cum on his hand. He wiped it on the comforter and undressed himself and laid down next to her. He had no idea where to start. Laying down, her feet only came down to his dick. So he decided to let her call the shots and asked, "How do you want it sexy?"

She laid down on her back and wiggled her index finger at him and said, "Come here!"

JC climbed on top of her and started to rub his dick against her pussy lips until it got hard. Once the warmth and wetness hit it, he grew harder and harder. He reached over and grabbed a condom from the table and slipped it on before slipping his dick into her hot box. He slid in slowly and felt her tense up and her little grip grew tighter against his arms with each inch he put into her. "Wait! Oh, shit! Wait!" she whispered, as he slowed his entry to accommodate her smaller size.

This was the tightest pussy JC had ever felt. "You want some more?" he asked when he noticed her facial expression. He looked down and saw he was only half inside her.

"Just...a...little more," she whispered, breathing harder. "Whooo! Jamie didn't tell me...oh fuck!" she screamed, as he slipped deeper into her. He stayed at that length and stroked her in and out until she was screaming like she was on fire. "Yes! Come on, yes!"

JC pushed his dick all the way in, stretching her apart until he hit the back of her pussy wall. Even though she was wet, her pussy stayed tight as he continued to beat it non-stop. Her pussy felt so good and was surprisingly scentless. It felt so amazing, he actually wanted to pull the condom off so he could really feel her.

Stephanie screamed her way to an orgasm and continued to take JC's dick while he pounded her like they were in a porno movie. He turned her on the side and fucked her even harder once he had more momentum. Stephanie was cumming like there was no tomorrow and there was white cream all over the sheath around his dick. JC took a chance and yanked the condom off, needing to feel her on him. She didn't seem to mind or notice as she reached down and guided him back inside her. Stephanie kept begging for him to fuck her harder, until she was shaking and holding his dick tightly with her pussy muscles. JC couldn't get his nut off, so after a while he turned her over and began fucking her doggie style. Since she was short he had to stand up on the floor while she was on the bed bent over. Instead of trying to back into him, she was trying to run from his dick. But JC grabbed her by the waist and kept her close, jamming his dick all the way in. "Fuck! Fuck! Fuck!" she shouted, cumming again almost immediately.

Sweat was pouring off JC's body as he neared his peak. Her pussy was squishy and wet, sounding like a lake when he finally pulled out and unleashed a torrent of hot cum onto her back where it dripped onto the sheets. Stephanie fell onto her stomach unable to say anything, trying to catch her breath. JC was tired too, but he had enough strength to get up and wipe his body and dick off. She laid there with his nut all over her and her own juices lingering on her pussy lips, "Your money is on the dresser," she finally said. "Let yourself out, I can't move right now. I'll call you soon baby."

JC took the time to shower and when he came out she was fast asleep in the same position he left her. He let himself out counting the money she left for him. Jamie called him about twenty minutes later and said, "Stephanie just called! She said you tore that pussy up like nobody ever has. She said she came over a dozen times before you even came yourself. You did good, she's a satisfied customer, now it's my turn!"

JC laughed as she told him what Stephanie had said, "Damn, girl! Can't a nigga even get an intermission?"

"Yeah, on your way over here you can rest! Hurry up!" she ordered him, hanging up the phone before he could say no.

When he got there, Jamie took him by the hand without a word, and fucked him until he was exhausted and could barely stand in the shower as she washed him off. He fell asleep on the bed wearing only a towel. When he woke up a few hours later, he saw Jamie was asleep next to him and he realized he wished it was Juicy. All this sex was draining his energy, energy he needed to be giving Juicy. He noticed Juicy had called while he slept and when he called her back she was in tears, seeing on the news about Kitten and Jason being dead. Juicy told JC she was on the way to his hotel. JC hurried up and got dressed, beating her there by fifteen minutes when she knocked on his door. He had to text Linda and tell her he couldn't make it tonight because something personal came up, she texted back that she understood and would text him another time.

JC rubbed Juicy's belly as she shared her feelings with him. "It's like everyone around me is getting killed! This shit's crazy! What's the world coming to?" she sniffled into the pillow, as he lay next to her listening.

JC held her tighter and replied, "Things happen to everyone for reasons no one knows. Just thank God nothing has happened to me or you. That's who is important right now. Everything is going to be okay."

"I love you JC! Thanks for listening to me. I'm sorry, I'm a mess right now. Please don't ever leave me or turn your back on this baby. We both need you."

"I'll never turn my back on you baby. I need the same from you too. I need to know you got my back, always," he said, looking her in the eyes just to let Juicy know he was serious.

"Pinky promise?" she asked, holding her pinkie out to him.

JC smiled and locked pinkies with her, "Alright, pinky promise."

"Can we move into the place sooner than we planned? My mom be trippin, treating me like a little girl and telling me what to do already wit the baby. I ain't trying to hear that shit! This is our baby, we choose what's going to happen."

"You under her roof Juicy. Let her be her."

CHAPTER 32

"*B*ut I don't have to be there JC. I'm helping her."

"Look, yall helping each other. She was okay before you, no matter if you helping her or not. Don't get impatient cause we got a little money. As you already seen, the tables can turn at any time. So be patient and stick to the plan."

"But-."

"But nothing Juicy. She's your momma, let her give the advice, she already been through it all. It's up to us if we take it, listening don't cost nothing. Stick to what we planned. We gonna be alright in a minute, okay? I promise," he vowed, kissing her on the forehead. Juicy kissed his lips and that eventually led to them stripping their clothes off and having sex for over an hour. They watched a movie after that, still naked in bed. Once the movie was over, JC got up and went into the bathroom.

When Juicy heard the shower turn on, she started snooping around. She looked in a couple dresser drawers, his pants and then looked around for his phone, but he had it in the bathroom with him, which she thought was suspicious. She made a mental note to look at it when he fell asleep. She wondered if he was in the bathroom texting someone else. She had noticed a change in his behavior, but she wasn't sure if it was her hormones changing because she was pregnant or if he was cheating on her or hiding some illicit behavior. He used to have sex with her more, but lately he only ate her pussy and when they did have sex he was more tired than usual and he nutted a lot less than he used to. She made her way back to the bed and was about to lay down when she lifted up the mattress to look beneath it. Underneath where he slept, she saw Jason's chain and bracelet. Tears sprung to her eyes and her mind started to think the worst. Juicy heard the water turn off, so she put everything back and laid down acting like she had dozed off while he was showering. All she could think of is that JC killed Kitten and Jason. Then she thought back to Gloria and wondered if he killed her as well. *What if the police were right about him, am I pregnant by a serial killer?*

She woke up early, not that she slept all that much or deeply. Instead of waking JC up, she left him a letter. She needed some time to get her thoughts together. Even though she no longer liked Jason, she did like Kitten and these were still human beings he had killed. She thought back to when JC said he wanted revenge, and how he asked her questions about her and Jason's relationship. *Was this his way of getting revenge?* She asked herself. Was he *capable of doing that?*

JC woke up around 8:30a.m. and noticed the letter at the foot of the bed. He reached down and read the note from Juicy.

Hey baby, I didn't want to wake you, so I left this note instead. I couldn't sleep because of all that's going on in my mind. I've lost so many friends in so little time and I haven't really gotten over Gloria being gone. I just need time to get my mind right and right now it's playing tricks on me and I don't want to take

*anything out on you. I love you so much JC and I can't wait
until we move into our new place. I am so stressed at my mom's
house, but what you said made sense and I need to stop stressing
about that part because it is temporary. I trust you when you
say everything will be okay and I can see how hard you're
working to make that happen. I'm with you in every way and I
would never stop loving you. Call me when you get up.*

Love you,

Juicy

JC couldn't help but smile after he read the letter. *My baby,* he
thought to himself as he checked his text messages. He had one
from Stephanie saying how good he was in bed. She told him
her insides were all sore and it would take her some time to get
used to his dick because she hadn't had anything that big
inside her. JC laughed and then listened to his messages and
saw that Linda had called at 8:00. He called her back, she
answered on the first ring. "Hi!"

"What's up? You called me?"

"Yes. Is everything okay?" she asked, sounding concerned or
worried.

"Yeah, everything is fine. Thanks for checking in."

"No problem, were you sleeping?"

"I'm up now, what you doing?"

"I'm in bed thinking about you. I'd love to see you if that's
possible."

"When?" he asked, thinking of how he could make it to see her.

"Now, I was hoping?"

He laughed at the desperation in her voice now.

"What? I wanted to see you last night," she reminded him gently, not wanting to push him away.

"Nothing, I'll be there in a couple of hours if you think you can wait that long."

"I can wait, you're worth waiting for. Hurry up and get here already!"

"Okay, bye-."

"JC?"

"Huh?"

"Can you stay all day with me? I leave on a trip in the morning, but I'll make it worth your while."

"Damn, Linda! I don't-,"

"$10,000 dollars?"

JC hesitated for just a moment before agreeing, "Okay, I'll be there shortly." He hung up and took a long shower. He needed that Ten G's. He drank two energy drinks on the way to Linda's place and she spent no time in leading him to the bedroom. They had sex off and on for several hours taking time out to shower together, eat, spread whip cream and chocolate on each other's body, until the clock struck midnight. After that, they cleaned themselves up again and then she changed the sheets while he sipped a glass of whiskey. When he fell asleep, he slept hard, satisfied that Juicy hadn't called and interrupted his plans because Linda really wanted him to stay. At around 3 a.m., Linda woke JC up by sucking his dick. He thought he was dreaming at first until he opened his eyes and saw her mouth sliding down his pole. After he came, she got up and took another shower.

JC fell asleep waiting for her to come out and when he awoke, she was putting her coat on. He got up to leave as well when she said, "No, relax. There's a spare key, the alarm code and your money on the dresser. Go to sleep and leave whenever you want to. I'll be back in three days. Come and go as you will. My daughter will be here, I let her know you'd be staying."

"You sure Linda? Your daughter doesn't know me. I don't want her to freak out and call the police."

"It's fine, I trust you. It's not a problem." Linda gave him a big kiss, gave his dick one last lick, and left in a hurry before she convinced herself to stay longer and be late for her plane.

JC was shocked by her hospitality, they had just met, yet she was trusting him with her most prized possessions, including her fine ass daughter. He fell back to sleep and was awakened about an hour with a knock on the bedroom door.

"Who is it?" he asked, pulling the sheet over his naked body.

"Me, Sandra. Can I come in?"

CHAPTER 33

*J*C took a shower and left at noon and went to Juicy's mom's house to drop off the money Linda had given him. "You gonna be okay?"

"No, I'm not! Where you going now?"

"A couple of states over. Trust me, I'll be back."

"When you leaving?"

"Tonight."

Juicy made JC take her to a fancy restaurant and to the movies since he was leaving her alone. She was acting weird, but he figured she was mad about him going out of town and probably the pregnancy was making her act all screwy. He dropped her back off at her moms and then he hit the road, leaving Atlanta by 10 p.m.

When Kelly got out of the shower, she found herself calculating how long it had been since she saw JC. Every time she thought of him, she was ready to find and kill him. She called Merido when she put her pajamas on.

"Merido, I need to talk to you," she said when he answered the phone on the first ring.

"Why? What's going on?"

"We need to get back to Atlanta and get this thing over with before the police get him or he comes after us. Remember what he did to the girls at the hotel before. He ain't gonna just forgive and forget."

Merido took a deep breath, "I know Kelly, but what do you want me to do? I have to go through my brother to find him. Lamoto put a hit on him on the streets and we still ain't close to finding him," he said, trying to make her see common sense before she just flew off the handle.

"Well, we have to figure something out. With us not being in Atlanta I feel helpless."

"Call me tomorrow. I'll call my brother tonight and try to figure something out, okay?"

"Fine, but if by tomorrow nothing happens, I'm coming up with my own plan."

"Do you want to speak to your mom?"

"No, I'll talk to her later. Just do your part, bye!" she said, hanging up on him before he could try to dissuade her. Sometimes she thought Merido had forgotten how dangerous JC was. She laid down, but couldn't fall asleep. She tossed and turned, seeing JC's face no matter how tightly she closed her eyes. Prior to everything happening, she had thought of expanding her business to Atlanta, but not while JC was still in the picture. She needed him dead, so she could purchase the house she saw online a few weeks ago. She gave up on sleep and went to sit at her computer. She went to JC's Facebook page and saw he hadn't been on in a while. Kelly probed deeper into his page and looked for his friends. She saw that a lady had posted a comment on one of his pics so she clicked on her page. She found a direct link to the Facebook page. Kelly had to put in her own username and password in order to access this lady's page. Kelly saw she was online right now and instant messaged her.

Kelly: Hi, I'm Kelly. A friend of JC's. Have you seen him lately?

Jamie: Yes, as a matter of fact I have.

Kelly: How long ago? I've been trying to get in contact with him for some time now.

Jamie: How did you say you knew JC?

Kelly: I'm married to JC's cousin and we have three kids together. JC's birthday is coming up and the kids want to surprise him with a party. So I thought I would track him down and schedule us a vacation down in Atlanta. But I don't want him to know, the kids are so excited!

Jamie: lol! Oh, okay. For a minute, I thought you was one of his little girlfriends. You know JC has all the women chasing his little butt. Here's my number. Call me so we can talk.

Kelly called her once she signed off, not believing her luck. "Hi, we just talked online."

"Hi, this is Jamie. How you doing girl?"

"I'm fine, how are you?"

"I'm good. So you want to surprise him? When's his birthday?"

"It's coming up in a little over a week. Like I said, the kids haven't seen JC in a while and when I mentioned his birthday they came up with the surprise party idea."

"I would love to help. JC and I are really good friends."

"Oh, really? That's cool?"

CHAPTER 34

"*A*re you in Atlanta?"

"No, but I can be, no problem. I'll bring his cousin and the kids. Can you help me find a venue for the party?"

"Absolutely, I know the perfect place at the hotel I'm staying at. I'll take care of everything, and don't worry, I won't ruin the surprise for you."

"Thank you so much Jamie. I'll call in a few days to touch base with you."

"Sounds perfect, thanks for telling me about his birthday, I'll have to find him a present."

After they hung up, Kelly was excited. She wanted to call Merido but decided to wait until morning to tell him. At least she was able to go to bed and fall into a contented sleep knowing that she was going to be able to get to JC.

JC drove to Pontiac, Michigan and headed to where Nino's mother had been living for more than twenty years. It was sunny out and nearly noon when he knocked on the door. When she saw who it was, she smiled, excited to see him.

"Hey Jason. How are you sweetie? Give momma some sugar, baby!"

JC smiled and leaned in to kiss her on the cheek. She was old and grey and had to use a walker to get around, but he saw her eyes were still bright and aware.

"Is Nino here?" he asked already knowing the answer.

"Nooo, Nino only comes home for the holidays sweetie. Come in and sit down. You want something to eat or drink? I cooked some mashed potatoes, corn bread, greens, and fried pork chops."

Remembering how great her cooking was almost tempted him, but he passed. "Nah, I'm okay. How's Gina been doing?"

"She's doing good. She deals with her brother a lot on different things."

"She get herself a man yet?"

"That girl ain't never gonna get a man. She too crazy. Ain't no man gonna put up with that."

"She still crazy, huh?"

"Yeah, that girl something else. I blame myself for letting her run with Nino and his friends instead of playing with the other girls."

"Where she living now?" JC asked.

She gave him two numbers to call and her address.

"You want me to call Nino and pass on a message for you?" she asked, reaching for her phone.

"Yeah, tell him this. Better yet, give him this," JC said, reaching under his shirt.

"Give him what baby?" she asked, expecting some money.

JC shot her in the chest three times and went out the door, as the neighbors were coming outside at the sound of gunshots. He drove over to the address she gave him for Gina. He didn't bother calling, giving her any advanced notice. He saw a green SUV in her driveway. He walked up to the door and knocked, wondering if Nino told her he had seen him in Atlanta.

"Oh my God! JC, hi!" she exclaimed, when she opened the door and saw him on the porch. She leaned out and kissed him on the cheek, almost recognizing him with his head shaved bald.

"How you been?" he asked, as she ushered him inside. The house was small, but clean, with newer furniture throughout. It was clear that Nino was sending his sister some extra bread or maybe she had her own hustle.

"I'm good. I've been real good actually. You know my brother make sure lil' sis eat."

JC laughed and said, "You right about that. He always did take care of family."

"How did you know where I stayed?"

"Your mom told me, I saw her before I came here. She tried to fatten me up with that cooking of hers. When I left, she was resting. She was bragging how your ass was still wild, so I thought I'd pay you a visit too while I was in the hood."

"Well, I'm glad to see you. How have you been? Did you get

all that police stuff handled? Boy, you know I'm still wild as hell and getting it in."

"Yeah, I'm straight. I got a court date next month. It's looking good."

"Well, good luck with all that," Gina said, going into the kitchen and began eating a fruit roll-up. She was thick, but a nice looking girl.

"Thanks. I was trying to call Nino about a couple of bricks, hoping he was in Michigan, but your mom's said he way down in Atlanta."

"He didn't tell you I had them?"

"His phone dropped out, so I didn't get the whole conversation."

"Yeah, I handle everything in Michigan for Nino."

"How much then, big time?"

"How many, roller?"

"Oh, you got it like that, huh?"

"I mean… I'm straight JC. Let me call Nino and see if I can get you a better price."

JC pulled out his gun as she reached for a cell phone. "That won't be necessary. Nino ain't gonna be answering no phone," he said, snatching the phone from her hand.

"You dirty muthafucka!"

"Yeah, whatever. Where the money and dope at?"

"You really gonna rob me, JC after all the time we been knowin' each other?" she whined, hoping he would show her some mercy.

"You can thank Nino when you talk to him."

"What did Nino do to you?"

"Bitch, I don't wanna talk! Where's the money at?" he demanded, slapping her across her mouth with the butt on his pistol. She dropped to her knees bleeding on the beige carpet. "Unless you want me to go pay your mama a different kind of visit?"

She knew he wasn't playing around and said, "It's…It's in the back room. Inside the closet," she cried out, spitting blood and teeth in her lap.

"Show me!" he ordered, kicking her in the stomach. "You make one wrong move, and you dead! You and your entire family!"

Gina got up holding her bruised stomach. She didn't think JC would kill her unless she did something stupid. He wouldn't risk pissing off Nino anymore than he was gonna be, she reasoned in her mind. With that thought in her head, she directed him to the money. "I can't believe you doing this JC."

JC snatched a pillow off the bed and used the pillow case to put the money and drugs in. The money was inside a safe, but the door was open like she had been in it recently or maybe she had gotten lazy. He grabbed stack after stack until the safe was empty. Then he stacked the bricks after the money, until there was no more room left. "You got a gym bag or something?"

Gina pointed in the back of the closet, but in her head she wanted to tell JC that Nino was gonna kill him, but she bit her tongue not wanting to give him a reason to kill her.

JC loaded the twelve kilos of cocaine into the gym bag, along with three kilos of heroin. "Where the rest at?"

CHAPTER 35

*S*he looked at him like he was crazy. "That's it! That's all I got!"

He took her at her word and said, "Thanks. Nice doing business with you."

He raised his gun and shot her twice in the face, one bullet entering her cheek bone and the other blowing out her left eye. Gina was dead before she hit the floor. He ran outside and threw everything into the trunk and headed to a hotel he used to go to in Auburn Hills.

———

Kelly had just hung up with Merido. She told him how she met one of JC's friends online and expressed the need to get to Atlanta ASAP. Merido stopped her from saying too much on the phones and made arrangements to meet at an out of the way restaurant in Southfield.

Kelly arrived first and ordered food for them, so they didn't get

interrupted by the waitress every five minutes. When Merido
got there, they began to talk about JC.

"So who is this friend of his and how do you know she won't
tell him?"

"She thinks I'm JC's cousin's baby mother."

"And?"

"I told her how JC's birthday was coming up and the kids
wanted to throw him a surprise birthday party. She's all for it,
even springing for the venue at her hotel.

"You told her his birthday was next week?"

"Yeah, why? What?"

"I don't trust it is what it seems. If she's such a good friend of
his, she should know his birthday. Don't you think?"

It hit her, what he was saying. "I didn't think about that.
Maybe she's a new friend of his? You think she could be
setting me up?"

"It's possible. So let's call my brother Lamoto, and find out
who you was chatting with. I'll have him check her out. He
could snatch her up and have her set JC up, you know what I
mean?"

"That sounds good, I just don't want to spook JC by snatching
her, especially if she's a close friend of his."

"I'd rather risk that then assume Jamie is with us."

"I can't believe I didn't think of that. I feel so stupid. I'm glad I
told you what was going on."

"Me too!" Merido said, raising his glass in a silent toast to what
was hopefully the end of JC.

After they ate, they both went their separate ways. Merido called Lamoto and gave him Jamie's phone number to trace to an address.

Before going home, Kelly drove out to Bay City to pick up the house money. Making plans in her head to still go to Atlanta because it was possible Jamie wasn't setting her up. When she got to the Bay City house she noticed all the girls were there sitting in the living room. Business was almost always slow that early in the day. It would slowly pick up throughout the day, and drive all the way into the early morning hours.

"I was hoping to catch most of you at one time," Kelly said, smiling at them.

One of the girls commented on the navy blue velour suit she had on. The jacket stopped right above her belly button. "You look super cute and comfortable."

"I am. I just bought it to wear around the house. Listen, why I have you all here I need to talk to you about something," Kelly started out, sitting on a bar stool. "I was thinking of expanding to Atlanta and taking all of you with me since you're already experienced. I'll understand if you don't want to move. I know some of you have regular clients and have families here too. Show of hands, who wants to go to Atlanta?"

With no hesitation all of the girls raised their hands. They knew with new territory meant new and more money, especially in the beginning.

"Good, better than I thought actually. Next week, I'm going to put in an offer on a nice house, eight bedrooms, six full baths, pool, hot tub, gym, movie theatre, the works. Wait until you see it, girls."

"You didn't take no pictures?" One of the girls asked excited to see their new home.

"I do have pictures of sorts, you can see a virtual tour online, come look," Kelly invited them to surround her while she went online with her phone. Kelly spent the next couple of hours going over her plans for the new house and slamming a couple shots of tequila with them to celebrate. On her way back home, she made a quick stop at the West Bloomfield house. She needed one more girl to move to Atlanta with her. Tonight, she would call up some girls that applied months ago to refill the Bay City house. She knew Atlanta would have plenty of competition, that's why she wanted her most experienced girls to come with her. When Kelly entered the house, she saw it was empty. She walked into the kitchen, looking for the yellow envelope, excited to see the house empty which meant they were busy at this time of day.

"Looking for this?" a familiar voice from the past asked her, sending shock waves through her body.

"JC?" she asked, turning around slowly. She almost passed out when she saw his face.

"Don't do anything stupid or I'll blow that pretty little face off, right here in the kitchen."

"How did-."

"No questions, please. We're beyond all that Kelly. I'm going to be the one asking the questions. Now drop that purse and turn around and walk backwards until you feel my hand on your back." She did as he said, dropping her purse to the floor and stopping when she felt his hand. He searched her carefully, removing the knife she had in a specially made sheath in her boot. He made sure to check her breasts as well since he knew she occasionally carried a small derringer pistol in her ample cleavage. He pulled a chair out for her and motioned with the gun for her to sit down.

CHAPTER 36

*K*elly sat down, feeling helpless and hoping one of her girls came in and heard what was going on and called Merido. She kicked herself for not hiring security for when the girls weren't here. She had no way to help herself out of this situation. She knew she couldn't beat him in a fight. He looked like he'd been working out. Now she understood what Marvin and Merido were saying when they told her she should have killed JC. She reflected back to when she shot JC. The scene replayed over in her mind, but she had developed feelings for him which is why she didn't kill him. Kelly thought he would leave and just never come back. She didn't want to be responsible back then for killing him.

"So tell me the connection you have with Merido?"

"Why should I tell you anything? You're just going to kill me, right?" she asked, looking him in the eyes.

JC smiled and walked up to her, caressing her face in his hand and then pulled it away only to have it return in the form of a punch right into her jaw. He felt her bones crack underneath the pressure from his knuckles, then he spit in her face to show the contempt he felt for her."Bitch, you gonna tell me every fucking thing I want to know," he shouted right in her face.

Kelly's face started to swell immediately, and blood leaked from her nose. She was about to reach for her blouse to wipe it but thought better of it.

"He's my step-father," she admitted honestly.

"Look how easy that was. As long as you tell me what I want to know, I might not send yo ass where you sent my baby mama. My first baby mama at that, you deceitful little bitch!" he screamed, slapping her with the butt of his pistol. Kelly fell out of the chair. "Get up, I'm not done with you yet!" he was so excited to see her, he didn't know what to do. He was consumed with rage and revenge, "Why did Merido want to kill me?"

"Money! It's always about money with him," she whispered holding onto the chair for support as blood leaked from the cut on her forehead.

"Who else was involved?" he asked, kicking her in the chest. She flew across the room into the counter.

"Marvin...Welma," she managed to eke out of her busted mouth.

"You know what bitch? You really had me fooled. You had me thinking you was so sincere and the whole time you was planning on killing me, you dirty bitch!"

"I knew I didn't kill you! I thought you would just leave and they would never find out! Marvin and Merido know I fouled up!" she said in between tears.

"What?" he asked, "What did you say?"

She was almost at the end of her strength when she said, "I

didn't want to kill you! I shot you in the shoulder on purpose, I love you, JC! I didn't kill your mom JC, I swear!"

"My mom?" JC was stunned. "She's dead?"

"Yes, she is and I didn't do it!" she cried.

JC ignored her denials. He would find out for himself who killed her. This was all about Kelly. "Where can I find Merido?"

"I don't know!" she said bracing for what she knew was coming next as a consequence to her answer.

JC got pissed and started pistol whipping her over the head repeatedly as she screamed for her life until he stopped. Blood was leaking from multiple gashes in her head and he was beginning to slip in the blood covering the floor from her wounds.

"Please JC! Please, I'm sorry! I spared your life, can't you find the love to do the same for me?" she asked, begging for her life. "I'll tell you what you want to know, if you promise just to kill him and not my mom or kids!" she said crying, as she crawled away from him, no longer begging for her life, but her children's.

"Where you going bitch?" he asked, grabbing her by the hair and throwing her against the wall. "Take this shit off!" he demanded, grabbing the hem of her pants. He snatched the pants so violently her legs flew into the air. With her pants out of the way he snatched her white thong and bra off, exposing her nakedness that was drenched in crimson. "Damn, bitch! You stopped shaving? Ain't no one been hittin' that shit?" he asked her.

She set with her back against the wall breathing hard. JC walked towards her and demanded, "Open them legs up!"

"Please JC!"

"SHUT...THE...FUCK...UP!" he screamed, while squatting down in front of her and sticking the barrel of his gun inside her pussy. He rammed it in and out of her like he did his dick when she was playing him.

"No, ahhh, stop! Please, stop!" she pleaded in pain as the cold metal rubbed against her dry vaginal walls. Tears mingled with the blood, creating a pinkish effect that might have been quite pretty if it wasn't from her own skin. Blood began to leak out of her pussy because of how hard he was jamming the gun in.

"You like that, bitch?" he asked, laughing maniacally as a foot caught him square in his nose, blinding him for a second as tears came to his eyes. The gun went flying somewhere behind him.

Kelly began crawling over him to get the gun, but JC snatched her by the leg, throwing her back against the wall. When his sight cleared a little, he began punching her in the back and ribs like she was a man. Kelly screamed for help until he punched her in the mouth, silencing her for a few seconds as the body blows could be heard outside the house. "Bitch, shut up!" he turned behind him and grabbed the gun and asked, "So you want to fight, huh? Get up then. I'll give you a chance!" he pulled her up by the hair and commanded, "Open your mouth!"

He tried to jam the gun in her mouth, but Kelly used her elbow to hit him as hard as she could right in the dick. "Aghh! You... bi-" JC yelled, as he fell to his knees, dropping the gun.

Kelly tried to run away, but JC tripped her and she hit her head on the edge of the marble counter, knocking her out. JC stumbled to his feet in pain as he slapped her awake, not letting her enjoy the sensation of not feeling the pain he was inflicting. She looked up at him, blood dripping from the many cuts on her face and head. He could hear how shallow her breathing was and he knew she had broken some ribs, one which had pierced her lung. It was time to put her down. He shot her in the stomach and watched her struggle to breathe, enjoying the fact that she would die slowly. To her credit, Kelly tried to still crawl away from him, but she didn't have the strength. JC easily stopped her and shoved the gun past whatever teeth she had left, and pulled the trigger. The gunshot splattered on the wall behind her and Kelly laid there, with her eyes fixed on JC, not blinking, just accusing him of not giving her the same chance she gave him, to live and start fresh somewhere else. But JC couldn't afford to take the chance that she would leave him alone. He stumbled out to his car hoping no one saw him, not that it mattered. They had to have heard the shouts and gun shots. Before he drove off, he realized in his rage he didn't get any info on Merido. He ran back inside and grabbed her purse from the floor before fleeing the scene.

CHAPTER 37

*W*hen JC turned onto the highway, he saw a police car flying past him at a high rate of speed with the sirens blaring. JC drove the speed limit, getting on I-75 and headed back to Atlanta. He wanted to be out of Michigan within two hours. He stopped at a rest stop when he got inside the Ohio state line and pulled out Kelly's phone to get Merido's number. Then he called Amanda, the girl he met at the phone store.

"Hello?" she asked not recognizing the number.

"Amanda, whatsup?"

The voice sounded unfamiliar to her, "Who's this?"

"JC, the nigga you-."

"Oh yeah, hi sweetie!"

"What you doing?"

"Waiting on you to give me a chance to show you how that phone works."

"You at work now?"

"I'm on my lunch break, why?"

"I need a big favor and I don't need any questions as to why."

"What?"

"I have a phone number, I need to track down the billing address."

"When do you need it?"

"ASAP! Like right now!"

"I'll go inside and call you back in ten minutes."

JC hung up and waited for her call. His stomach was churning so much he opened the door and vomited outside the car. He had flash backs of killing Kelly. He heard his phone ring and he thought it was Amanda, but Juicy was calling him. He picked up and told her he'd call her back in a few minutes. Then Sandra called.

"What's up?"

Without any preliminaries she said, "JC, I'm pregnant. You got me pregnant!"

"It ain't mine!"

"What you mean it ain't yours? You think I'd be calling you if it wasn't yours? It's yours and I'm keeping it. I don't need you for anything so don't think I'm trying to get you on the hook or something. I just thought you should know."

"Sandra, I can't have that baby."

"Why?"

"Because I have a baby on the way already."

"JC relax. You don't have to worry about anything. You know my mom and dad are rich."

"That's not the point, Sandra. "

"Then what?"

"Look, I have to call you back," he told her, clicking over to Amanda's call.

She gave him the address and he quickly hung up on her, promising to come see her soon. There was so much shit going on right now, he barely had time to think about any of them. Now that he had Merido's address, he promised himself to pay him a visit. He drove to Atlanta, knowing he had been gone long enough from Juicy. It wouldn't be long before his baby girl was born. He drove straight through and finally called Juicy back after he relaxed his mind with some music.

"Damn, it took you long enough to call me back."

"I'm sorry baby, it's this damn traffic. I'm trying to get home to you, but there's a lot of cars in my way. I love you!"

"Ugh, you getting on my last nerve!"

"Chill out, I'm on my way. Pack everything up. I got a surprise for you. You're coming with me."

"Where we going?"

"You'll see," he said, excited about all the money and drugs he had. There was enough to take care of them for a while. "Trust me!"

"How long you gonna be JC?"

"A few more hours. I'll call you when I get closer." Juicy didn't respond and he said, "Juicy? You there?"

"Huh?"

"What's wrong? Everything okay?"

A. ROY MILLIGAN

Juicy couldn't respond all she could do was cry. JC just held the phone until she was done. "You ready to tell me what's wrong with you? This pregnancy got you trippin'." Each time he asked her what was wrong, she started crying again. "Damn it, Juicy! What's wrong?" he asked again.

In between sniffles she said, "Nothing. I love you, JC."

"I love you too baby."

"Just call me when you get close," she said between sniffles.

"Okay," he said into the phone and hanging up before she started crying again. He didn't have time for this emotional ass shit she was feeling. JC had finally reached the Atlanta city limits sign. He called Juicy and told her he was about twenty minutes away. He drove to her mom's house, happy that Kelly was finally out of the picture and soon so would Merido and his brother. He shook his head remembering how she tried to fight back. JC had to give her credit, she fought more than some niggas he killed.

When he got to Juicy's street, he called to tell her to come outside, but she didn't answer. When he pulled into the drive way, the door opened. She stood there with tears in her eyes as she looked at him. JC waved his hand for her to come to the car, but she shook her head and mouthed the words, "I'm sorry!"

Seconds later, he heard the reason as police cars came flying at him from every direction and he heard the rotors of a helicopter above him. Two cars blocked him from behind and two officers with police dogs stood on either side of the car with their guns drawn.

Juicy had called the police after she found Jason's jewelry. She knew JC had done it. The police told Juicy that JC would get natural life if she helped capture him instead of the death penalty. At least then he would see his daughter. She fell to her knees as she watched the car get surrounded. She saw the murderous look in JC eyes when he stared at her. He would never understand how torn she was in what she did, but she wanted her daughter to have a chance at a normal life, not waiting for the police or goons to hunt him down, maybe killing all of them.

"Bitch!" JC yelled as he floored the pedal staight into the garage door, going right through it. He then started firing at the police as he got out the car running into the house after Juicy.

Shots rang out but slowed down when JC was out of site. Police knew Juicy and her mom was inside and they didn't want to accidently shoot them.

JC got into the house and Juicy ran out the house towards the police, and JC was right behind her firing shots at the back of her head, two shots piercing her back. But he was quickly gunned down. The police filled his body up with over 30 bullets and they both layed in the front yard lifeless….

Thank you for reading, don't forget to leave a review.

Women Lie Men Lie Part 4 in stores now

Books by A. Roy Millgan

Women Lie Men Lie Part 1
Women Lie Men Lie Part 2
Women Lie Men Lie Part 4
Women Lie Men Lie Part 5
Fifty Shades Of Snow Part 1
Fifty Shades Of Snow Part 2
Fifty Shades Of Snow Part 3
Naive To The Streets
Stack Before You Splurge
Girls Falls Like Dominoes

Self Help Books
From Prison To The Publishing Game
From Prison To The Car Hauling Game

Made in the USA
Monee, IL
21 November 2024

70795399R00125